about the author

Anne Bailey was born in Woking in 1958 and went to school in Surrey. She has done a variety of jobs, including farm and factory work, and has spent some time on a kibbutz in Israel.

She always wanted to write, but her first book, *Scars* was not published until 1987, but was quickly followed by *Burn Up*, *Rhythm and Blues* and, recently, *Israel's Babe*. Her other interests are music, films and reading about psychiatry. She lives in a mobile home in Surrey and has her own transport – a Kawasaki 200cc motorbike.

Rhythm and Blues

ANNE BAILEY

faber and faber

LONDON · BOSTON

First published in 1990
by Faber and Faber Limited
3 Queen Square London WC1N 3AU
This paperback edition first published in 1993

Printed in England by Clays Ltd, St Ives plc

Anne Bailey is hereby identified as author of this work
in accordance with Section 77 of the Copyright, Designs
and Patents Act 1988

A CIP record for this book is available from the British Library.

ISBN 0 571 16839 6

2 4 6 8 10 9 7 5 3 1

To Roger and Chris Robins,
For inspiration and for being there

Chapter 1

We had a party.

We had such a damn fantastic party, me and my mates.

In my father's luxurious home.

It was great. Dad went out at eight. My friends came in at nine and what a rave-up we had.

Most of us were blazing drunk. But could I give two hoots? Could I really? Not two hoots. It was great. Wine spilt on the carpet. Glasses smashed. People making love on whatever free bed they could find. Including me. Including me. It was all so way out and fantastic.

I got rid of them at two. My brother came in half an hour later when I hadn't quite managed to clear all the mess up.

'I don't believe it,' he half screeched.

'Oh, get lost.'

'You bitch.'

'Yeah, OK. I love you too, brother.'

'Why bother clearing up? Why not just leave all the mess for Dad to see? That's what you want isn't it?'

'My deed has been done, darling. Get back to your life of acting and leave my life alone. We're miles apart, Adrian. Let's leave it, shall we?'

'I'll thump those wallies. So-called mates of yours.'

'You couldn't thump a caterpillar. All mouth. No guts. That's your trouble.'

'Spoilt bitch.' He turned to go. His words had speared me, though. So I had to turn. Have my last say.

'Yeah? And what the hell are you?' I screamed. 'Smarmy, creepy, he-man, or rather, boy. Who'd call you a man? You don't even know what it's meant for, do you? You don't even know where to put the damn thing. Didn't Mummy teach you that before she found her freedom?'

She found her freedom.

She found her freedom.

She found her freedom.

Echoing around the kitchen. Echoing. I was staring at the door which Adrian had slammed in my face. Three-thirty in the morning. The party had been good. The party had been good.

'Hell!' I half shouted. I swung round and thumped the table. Hell, what's going on? In me. Something. Like a torrential rainstorm. Give me a break. An umbrella. Put it up inside me. Scream. Scream. Scream. Christ, I feel like screaming. He'd spoilt it, of course. Adrian always spoils it. Nothing seemed so good after he'd had a go at it. Guilt. Pouring into my very veins. Instead of blood. Transfusion. Give me a transfusion. To keep that pure hatred going. That pure hatred.

I went into my bedroom. Well, more of a flat than a room. All my own amenities in there. Even a loo. Three rooms. Laid out. Spaced.

I sat at my drum set. Just tapping away. Pulled the mike to me. Oh yes, I was up on stage. Thousands of people watching me. Getting into the beat. Fast beat. Let me flow. That adrenalin. Like swimming down a fast-flowing river. No safety harness. Give me danger. Give me excitement. What else? What else?

Then, then, just then that thought came into my mind. The kids. Dad's kids. Dad's kids. Think later. Think later. Not now. Now I'm just so damn pissed off.

2

Bang. Bang. Bang. On the drums. Make a noise. Drown out the thoughts. Sing a song. Play the drums. I'm talented. Like my father was once. I wish to hell I hadn't cleared up after the party. I wish to hell I hadn't.

Spoilt bitch.

Words drowning out the rhythm. Words in my mind. In large black painted letters.

Spoilt bitch.

Chapter 2

It isn't fair. Nothing in this lousy world is fair. Is it? I mean, is it? Can you honestly say this society we live in is fair? Who can? Put your hands up and kiss my arse. Count to ten. Tra la la. No, it's not a fair world. Actually it's really bad. Bad. I don't want to know, you see. I don't want to know about Dad's other kids. I couldn't care if they're in a home. What a family. What a crack, that is. We're all crazy. Delinquents. Cracking up. I mean, Dad's screwed so many women it's a damn miracle he's got any manhood left. Big he-man that he's been since coming out of prison. He went in for drugs. You know, possessing drugs. He spent four months in there. Well, what do you do when you're forty-nine and put in jail? What do you do? You turn to that big man up in the sky and subsequently become a law-abiding citizen. A family man. You wish to become a saint. With a halo of light above your head. Creeps. Creeps. It gives me the creeps. I mean, it's crazy, he's really changed since being inside. I mean, for a start he's kept the same girlfriend for eight months. And he's been faithful to her. Faithful! I mean, what does that mean? He's just so perfect now. He does everything right all of a sudden. You know, right on. He's turned into a right, proper father. Church on Sunday and all that crap. I mean, what is a girl of sixteen expected to do? I mean, Dad used to be great. He took me with him everywhere. We had fun. Wild parties. Booze. All the outrageous people of his half-bit band. And others. He had woman after

4

woman. He was the stud all right and I was proud of him. I was the only kid of his who actually lived with him. Darling Adrian, we mustn't forget him, he lived with Mum. But me, no way. Me and Dad were together. Right and royal together. I used to go on his gigs with him. Watch him work. It was great. He gave me everything. Anything I wanted. But most of all he gave me excitement. God, he could make my adrenalin go. Burn. On fire. Yeah. Wow. Those were the days, were they not the days. Sure. Christ, I've lived and I'm only sixteen. Don't think of the past. It only makes the present seem even more unbearable. Unbelievable more like. Unpresentable. To me. So, I have a wild party, ruin the house, and all my problems go away? No, of course not. I just like it. Like the fear. Getting the old adrenalin going again. Just in case he'd walked in and found us. Just in case. Now, that would have been a laugh. Spare the rod, spoil the child. Well, that's what it says in the Bible, doesn't it? And he's such a Bible creeper these days. Surely he must take it literally. Huh, I'm not scared of him. Touch me, Daddy, and I shall show you what a real tyrant I am. Just like you used to be. Just like that. In fact I'm surprised he didn't father more than four kids. The stud, yeah!! I must have been kidding myself thinking that. He's only fathered four of us. But the kids in the home are illegitimate. They come from the same woman. She died. Committed suicide. Well, now Dad has this weird idea of getting custody of the two kids and getting them to come and live with us. Me, him and Adrian. Oh, what a dream. Them returning home to Daddy. Sure, it's going to be as easy as that. They'll want to come running back to him, of course. Just like that. Running back to the saint. The two girls. Returning to the saint. I don't know, though. He has kept in touch with them. Yer know, but sometimes Dad just has this knack of getting everything he wants. Like especially now. He's got a sort of aura about him. Positive and powerful. As if he knows exactly what he's doing and where he's going. Just exactly on the right path forward. Hell, sometimes that real scares me. He doesn't care about me like he used to. He doesn't, he's changed. He's definitely changed.

Chapter 3

A few weeks later he gained custody. I was told they could come and live with us for weekends just for a trial. I had another party. Just because of that. I just had to do something. My property. Keep your damn hands off. He's my father. Shit, it all makes me sick. Today's Thursday. They're coming tomorrow night. The two girls. What the hell. I'm buggered if I know what's going on. Whatever it is, though, I don't like it. And it makes me feel real damn angry.

'What's wrong?' Dad asked.

'Nothing.'

'You're not eating.'

'No.'

'I thought you liked beef.'

'It depends who cooks it.'

'You don't want it?'

'Why don't you tell me about all the starving people in the world? And that I'm lucky I'm not one of them.'

'Oh, turn it off, Matti.'

'Piss off, Adrian.'

'Mattianna!'

'Adrian's hopeless at cooking, Dad.'

'Well, you can cook tomorrow then.'

'I won't be here.'

Dad looked at me. His craggy face puzzled.

'I'm going to stay with Jamie.'

'No you're not.'

'Dad, I'm going to stay with Jamie.'

'I'm telling you love, you're not. I'm not giving you permission to go and stay with Jamie.'

'You can't stop me.'

'You go and you won't come back.'

'Thanks. That's all I wanted to hear. Can I be excused?'

'NO. You can wait there.'

'What's up with you?'

'Don't start that again.'

'I want to go to the loo.'

'Bullshit.'

'Christians aren't meant to swear.'

'Who said so? You're in touch with God, are you?'

'Yeah. I'm sitting right next to him.'

'You know, I've been patient, Matti. Why don't you talk about what's troubling you? I've asked you until I'm blue in the face.'

'Nothing's troubling me. It's not me.'

'OK. So, I've been patient. But you've gone far enough. Next time, watch it. You know what I mean.'

'Are you going out tonight, Dad? For a bit of the old smack?'

'D'you want me to hit you?'

'I just asked a question.'

'OK. Adrian, I'll need a hand after dinner. With Matti's drums.'

I jumped. His words stinging. Burning.

'What?'

'I know a kid who wants some drums.'

'What d'you mean?'

'I bought them. I'll sell them.'

'My drums?'

'Not any more.'

'You're winding me up.'

8

'No, I'm not. I've warned you enough.'

I could hardly believe he'd spoken. He'd said those words. It was like I was trying to blot them out.

'Wind up. Wind up. Wind up,' I said.

'OK. Come on Ade, food can wait. Find the keys in my jacket pocket and go and get the van. Bring it round to the front.'

'OK, Dad.'

I followed him. All the way up the stairs to my room. I stood behind him as he started taking my drum kit to bits. It suddenly sunk in.

'Dad!'

'What?'

'They're my drums. I mean I play in a band. Our drums. The drummer, you know. Christ, Dad.'

He didn't answer. Just unscrewed the kit. Piled it into separate piles. I suddenly started to panic.

'Dad, I'm sorry, OK? I won't wind you up no more, honest. I won't. Honest. Just don't get rid of the drums. I love them. It's the only thing I'm good at.'

'You'd better start being good at something else then.'

'This is unbelievable. I haven't even done anything wrong. What have I done? It's not fair. I won't wind you up again, I said. You're just jumping down my throat. It's not fair.'

'You won't do it again? Ruin the house when I'm out? Go to bed with any Tom, Dick or Harry.'

'I never did that.'

'OK, Ade, start taking it out.'

'You dare touch those drums. You creepy bastard.'

'I won't have that language in this house. You don't talk to your brother like that.'

'I didn't sleep with *anyone*. Adrian told you that. It's not true. He always splits anyway.'

'I could have handled it if you'd kept your mouth shut at dinner. But no, you have to push me, don't you? Push. Push. Push. No more, Matti. You've got to start learning.'

'I know everything. I don't need to learn. You need to learn. You don't know anything. Think your kids will come running after you. They hate you. I'm the only one you've got. You pissed on the rest of them, didn't you?'

'Yeah, I pissed on the rest of them. But they seem to know a damn sight more than you know. They've got sense, you know, sense, up here. They know right from wrong. My mistake. I forgot to teach you. You're just ignorant. Mouthy. Bitchy. It's going to stop. If I have to strip this room, it's going to stop.'

'I'm getting out of this place, anyway. I hate it.'

'You'd better get out then. Get yourself a job.'

'That's what you want. Me to go. That's what you want.'

'Yeah, at the moment I'd love it. You give me a pain in the neck.'

'OK, I'll keep the drum set and I'll go.'

'You haven't got the guts to leave here. You haven't got the guts. I'll tell you something else. I love all my kids. You've got to learn to share. I made lots of mistakes but I'm putting them right.'

'You owe me.'

'How?'

'You took me away from Mum. Now she's dead. I never got to know her. You owe me. Don't forget that.'

'I owe you a good thrashing.'

'You swear at me, don't you? I bet you won't swear at them. You can't change. You try. But you're still a pig at heart.'

'One more word from you and the hi-fi goes as well.'

'Why don't you take my whole room? Think I care. I don't care. Presents from you. Shit from you, that's all they were.'

'Come here.'

'I'd rather not get near, thanks very much.'

I tried to fight him off when he suddenly lunged at me. He grabbed me and had hold of a large chunk of my hair. He dragged me to my bathroom and actually shoved a bar of soap in my mouth. Awful it was. Bloody nearly made me sick. And I was nearly choking because his hand was over my mouth and nose, keeping the soap there. My face was hurting where his nails were digging in and I suddenly felt deflated. All my anger had gone. I suddenly felt scared. Lonely. Afraid. I was aware of the tears coming down my face.

He eventually let me go and I spat the bar of soap out. I felt really sick and was crying and I just slid down the wall of the bathroom and cried into a towel. I moved when I suddenly remembered my hi-fi.

I shot back into my room. Just as Dad and Adrian were carrying it out.

'Dad?'

'What?'

'What's happening. That was my Christmas present.'

'If you're good you can have the hi-fi back after a month.'

'What about the drums?'

'You'll have to save up for a new set. Get a job. It won't take long.'

I turned away from them and went back into the bathroom. I washed out my mouth with cold water. I did it again and again and again. Trying to get rid of the taste. Hell's bells. I looked in the mirror. What's going on, baby? What's happening? What is happening?

'Matti?' It was Adrian, later on.

'Dad hates me.' And like a stupid earhole I started crying again.

'You know that's not true.'

'I don't want them kids here.'

'Come downstairs, come on,' he said. 'You can't do anything about your drums. It's all over. Come on, wash your face. I'll make us a cup of coffee.'

'You don't know what it's like to be hated.'

'Don't talk daft. Come on, wash your face.'

'Adrian?'

'Em?'

'Do you love me?'

'Yeah. I love you.'

'I bet you'll love those kids more than you love me.'

'Don't be stupid. You've just got to show Dad, OK? Show him that you're grown up now. In a constructive way. Show him. I'll go and make the coffee.'

Chapter 4

Sure, I can survive everything. Sure. I've got that much confidence, haven't I? That's why I always worry now. Worry about whether my spots show. Worry about whether I've got bad breath. Worry as to how I sound. I worry that I'll never make it big. I worry that I'll be left alone, with no one. Alone in this large, great, unfair world. Yeah, I don't know what the hell's come over me. Everything seems so morbid. I worry about Mum too. Although she's dead. I worry that she doesn't love me. Didn't love me. Then I feel guilty because I wasn't home. Sometimes I wished she didn't love me. Then I wanted her to. I wish she hadn't died. I don't really want Dad to get married again to his new girlfriend. Oh, I've got nothing against her really. At least she's older than his other girlfriends. She's more Mum-like in a way. Her husband died. She's got three daughters. She's a nurse.

Yeah, well, I love to think of Mum being back again. Perhaps she's watching me now. And then I feel jealous of Adrian for having had Mum and me not. Now, he's got Dad as well. Sometimes I wish he hadn't got Dad. Yeah. I missed out on Mum. So he should miss out on Dad. That's what I reckoned. I feel hard done by.

I looked at the space where my drum kit had been. Cope with it. In a constructive way. I went to my wardrobe and took out my guitar. Sure. Sure. My drums, I loved. My drums I loved. But I can still sing songs. Write songs. I can play the guitar and compose as well as playing drums. Cor, real talented, that's me. I'll be constructive. What the hell about the band, though? How am I going to explain it away to them. The band? Sure, well. We are a band. When everyone remembers to turn up for rehearsals. When everyone remembers to do that. We haven't had any gigs yet. They're not serious enough, really. They don't work at it. I don't know. That's the trouble, yer see. I just don't seem to know anything about anything any more. I used to be so sure. So confident. Even when Dad was in prison. I didn't worry that much. I thought it would be the same when he got out. All be the same. Huh, that's a laugh. The best laugh out. The same? Sure.

I took my small radio cassette player out of a cupboard and plugged it in. Well, I guess that would have to do for the time being. A month, he'd said. A month, if I was good. It was like being four years old again. Four years old. Although I always got what I wanted when I was four years old.

I suddenly remembered about the coffee Adrian was making so I quickly dashed down the stairs and found him in the lounge with it.

'Thanks, Ade.' I curled up on our round settee. 'Are you seeing Natalia tonight?' I asked him.

'No, not tonight.'

'Is she working late? Doing overtime?' His girlfriend works in the same factory as Dad. In the offices there.

'Yeah. There's a rush order on at the moment.'

'I s'pose I'd better get a job,' I said.

'You!'

I looked at him. 'You don't have to sound so surprised.'

'Well, you've been sitting on your arse for five

14

months, since you left school. Which you were only at for a year anyway. You've been sitting on your arse.'

'Sure, I know.'

'So, why now?'

I shrugged. 'I want another drum set. That's my whole life, Ade. I can't live without a drum set. I'm going to start a new band. Get in with someone, you know? So I need to get a job. Then I can leave home.'

'Leave home?'

'Yeah.' I tried to keep a serious face but Adrian was looking at me. Pulling all grumpy faces. In the end I covered my face with my hands and blew a raspberry. 'OK, so?'

'Get told off by Daddy for the first time in your life and you want to leave home. That's life, girl. That's how you learn. Right from wrong. You know. Respect. Manners. You need them to live. Be wise like Mum. Don't run out just because he punished you. Don't run out. That's the coward's way.'

'It's not just that, though. It's everything. My whole life is so different now. And those kids are coming tomorrow. It's going to ruin us. It really is. What does he expect? Us to be really nice to them. Accept them, just like that, as if they're part of the family.'

'They are part of the family. They're his daughters. That makes them half sisters to us. They are part of the family. You've got to accept that.'

'He's only doing it because he feels guilty.'

'No, he's doing it because he feels love for them. He's going to try to be a proper father.'

'And where does that leave me? Out in the cold. I knew him how he was before. That was the real him.'

'I understand that. It's hard for you. More than for any of us, I guess. I understand that, Matti.'

'Try explaining it to him.'

'He does understand, but just lately you haven't given him a chance. You've been so rude and bolshie to him. He's wanted to talk to you about it but you won't. You won't.'

'Why should I? Why should I? Make it easy for him. That's what he's expecting. Everyone to make it easy for him. Well, that's not on. It's hard for me. Let him see how it feels.'

'It's been hard for all of us. Maybe more for you. It was hard for me and the girls. We've all got our problems, Matti. But if you can't talk them through, you might as well go and lock yourself in a cupboard. And throw the key away. You've got to give it a chance.'

'OK, so it's all my fault.'

'It's your fault you got your drum kit and stereo taken away. That was your fault. He doesn't do things without a good reason.'

'OK, I was a naughty little girl. Well, that's his fault, he brought me up.'

'Sure. And you're still five years old. Come on, Mattianna, you've got to grow up. Take some responsibility for your life.'

'OK. OK. Shut up, you've had your lecture time.'

'See, off you go again. You won't take any advice. You don't want to listen. How come you have to make it hard for yourself. All the time. It's like you're committing social suicide.'

'Oh, that's good. Name of a song. Social suicide. I don't know what the hell it means but it's good.'

'It means you've got to start looking out for other people rather than it being number one all the time. You know, straight up. I've got a lot I could hate you for if I wanted it to be like that.'

I looked at him.

'Think about it, without getting ratty. Now, pass the paper. I want to see what's on telly.'

I threw the paper to him and moved to our pine, swinging hammock which was down one side of the lounge.

I felt right fed up. I mean, really. Thinking of what he'd said. Wanting to forget his words but somehow they kept writing themselves on my mind. Oh yeah, I'm the bolshie, ratty and, according to Dad and Adrian, the ignorant one. The ignorant one. One. Me. Think about yourself. Number one. Selfish fart.

I blew another raspberry just as Ade turned the telly on. He hit me on the head as he went back past me. I just lay there, though. Making the hammock swing. Thursday. One more day and they'll be here. Two of them. For the weekend. If that goes OK there'll be a week. If that goes OK they'll be here for good. I declined to blow another raspberry. I put my hands over my face. I could hear movement in the kitchen. Sure, Dad's back. After getting rid of my drum kit and my hi-fi. How the hell was I meant to act? As pleased as punch? Sure. I can do that all right. I'm so damn wise. Ho. Ho. Ho. That's a laugh. And when I think about being wise I think about my mother, don't I.

Tears crept down in between my fingers. How come sometimes I miss her so much? After all, it has been nine months now. Nine months. Why the hell didn't I cry at the funeral? Why didn't I grieve over her death? Why? I'd never missed her, but I miss her now. There are days I wake to find my heart in my feet and a sinking feeling. Mum. Mum. Mum. Where were you all my life? Where were you? Why did I just toss you aside as if you didn't exist? Why didn't you insist I stayed at home with you and the others. So many whys in my mind. Questions. Questions. Questions.

I heard Dad come in but didn't move my hands away from my face. I was still crying and I didn't want anyone to see me. I heard Dad's voice. Talking to Adrian. It was OK. It was all OK. He sounded pretty normal. Normal. I didn't want him to stay in the lounge, though. I felt tense all of a sudden. Tense. I cursed when the talking continued. When he asked what was on telly and sounded as if he wasn't intending departing from the lounge. I cursed. Through my hand. What a crust. I can't even move in my own home. Stuck like a statue. Stuck.

Chapter 5

I stayed like that, for what seemed like ages. Then Dad eventually went out to do the washing up. So I moved. Take yer chance, girl, when yer can.

I went through the back door of the lounge to go up to my bedroom. It looked so empty without my drum kit and hi-fi. So empty. I lay on my bed and closed my eyes. I fell asleep and woke at ten to ten when there was a tap on my door.

'Matti?'

I turned over and pulled the pillow over my head. I didn't want Dad. Half a bleeding sleep. Fed up. I didn't need Dad. But he turned my light on.

'Come on, wake up, Matti. Ade and I are going for a drink. D'you want to come.'

'I'm asleep.'

'I want you to come.'

'Sure.' I sat up in bed. Looked at him. In his thick white jumper. Grey hair. Slightly podgy face. He'd put on weight over the past months. Since he'd come out of prison. Put on weight. Not so much the stud any more. Looks wise anyway. Not that he ever has been, really. He's just got that sort of aura about him. That aura. I noticed it again then. Not that it's a thing which comes and goes. It's always there but sometimes, like, you just sort of take it for granted. And not really notice it.

'Come on, we'll go out for a swift drink, then we can come back and have a chat.'

'Sure.'

'Sure, yeah. That's right.'

Why do I start crying. At the most stupid times. It's like someone just turns the tap on. At any given time. Turns the tap on. I turned away from him. Flung my legs over the side of the bed.

'D'you want to talk now?' He came round to my side of the bed. Rested his hand on my head. 'Matti?'

'I don't know what's wrong with me.'

'No.'

'Oh, forget it. I'll get changed, OK? I'll come out for a drink. I'll get changed.'

'That's my girl.'

'Not any more,' I mumbled.

'I am capable of loving you just as much as the others, you know. They won't stop me from loving you.'

'Don't take any notice of me. I'm just a bolshie, ignorant, ratty, bitch. Yes. You said so. Don't forget, you said so.'

'I want to make it work, Matti. For all of us. If only you'd talk. Tell me.'

'How can I when I don't know.'

'You don't want them to come?'

'It's your choice.'

'It's not a choice.'

'We used to have real good times. Real good times. It's all different now.'

'And you have to adjust. Build up a new life for yourself. You can't centre your life around me. Get out. Meet new people. New friends. Friends that stimulate you. Not like the crowd you've been hanging around with just lately. They're not interested in music. They're just interested in having a good time.'

'I miss Mum.'

'I know.'

'I don't want anyone else in this house. We work well together. All of us do. It won't be the same. Everything always has to change. I want it to stay the same.'

'They're good girls, Mat. They've got problems but they're all right underneath. You can help them. They need us. I know it's a hard time for you. But you've just got to buckle down. Get on with it. Concentrate on your dreams. You need a job, though. To get into a routine. I've given you enough time to sort yourself out.'

'Can I work at the factory?'

'D'you want to?'

'Is there a job?'

'I gave you a chance on that six months ago. You walked out after a month.'

'That was just cleaning, though.'

'There might be a few jobs coming up. I'll look into it. I want you to promise me something, though.'

'What?'

'If I get you a job there, you'll make a go of it. Try to get on with the other people working there. You know what I mean. You've got to start at the bottom and work your way up. That's the only way to do it. A gutsy job. But it'll give you some independence. Your own money. You've got to stick at something in the big, old world.'

'I still want to make it in music though. That's my dream.'

'OK. So work at it. Get rid of that motley crew. Your so-called friends. And get some more people in. You've got talent, I know. You're a good singer.'

'I'm a good drummer.'

'Yes.'

'But I haven't got them any more.'

'You know why.'

21

'That was a bloody thing to do.'

'Tit for tat. You treat me bad, I'll treat you bad.'

'Yeah, well. You never used to be like that.'

'No. I used to spoil you. I was wrong. I'm sorry I did it now. You had an insecure life with me. It wasn't a proper life. I shouldn't have let you stay with me.'

'I wanted to.'

'I know. But now you've got to accept I've changed. I want a different life.'

'Are you going to sing again?'

'I don't know yet. But none of the high life any more. I learnt my lesson by being put inside. That was a hard lesson to learn. I want something good to come out of that lesson. I'm going to try by putting my family first now. Other people before me. You've got to learn to do that too. We've got to pull together. We can all sort it out. But we've all got to work at it. And you've got to work at something too. For your life. Work towards that dream. But even if you are successful you could still throw it all away. If you haven't had the right grounding. I want to give you that right backing now. It's not too late. And if that means teaching you lessons, then that's the way it's got to be. Try to understand, Matti.'

'Yeah.'

'Try to understand.'

'OK.'

'You've got to stop the language and the back chat. We used to talk like that but if I let you get away with it, what will the other kids expect. Anyway, it's not the right way to go on, is it?'

I looked down at my hands.

'You know, Matti. You know deep down. Come on, get changed quickly and come down. We'll go out.'

'OK.'

'Smile then.'

I looked at him and he winked at me. I guess I smiled, sort of.

'Hurry up then, Matt.'

I suppose yer could say he was something. Something, yer know. I guess I still loved him. Still loved him. Who knows anyway? He's not a bad old boot. He used to be a good singer, anyway. I hope he sings again. I like seeing him on stage. And at least no one can slag him off any more for his lifestyle. They can't do that. One up to the world. You can't slag my Dad off. Although he was a pig to take my drum kit away. It's OK for me to slag him off, but no one else can. You know, I used to cry when I heard someone say something bad about him. It used to break my heart. In spite of everything, the way he behaved and all that, I used to think he was perfect. A saint. Sure. I used to think that. I was never disillusioned by him. My hero to the end. My hero. Hell, get up, Matti, girl. Get up. Get changed. Go out. So I had a party without telling him. I suddenly felt guilty and ashamed, about that. Trust Adrian to grass. All mouth, no guts, Adrian. I sort of felt guilty, though. Just because I think he'll prefer those other kids to me. His other daughters. You know, at the moment I'm the only girl at home and in a way I like it that way. I get all the attention. From Adrian and Dad. You know, it's just that with two other girls coming. One a year younger than me and one a year older. Well, Dad's bound to love them just as much as he loves me. That's what I can't cope with. I want all the attention all the time. All right, I admit it. I admit it. I like rowing and backchatting and everything else because I get attention that way. I mean if I was just quiet as a mouse and had no lip, then, hell, no one would pay me any attention. No one would at all. Then where would I be? I couldn't have that. No way. No way.

Chapter 6

It turned out to be quite good over our local pub. We went in Dad's Mercedes and went in the lounge bar. It wasn't overcrowded but there were enough people to create a good atmosphere. I put some records on the juke box while Dad was getting in the drinks and Adrian found somewhere to sit.

All in all, after the bad start to the evening it didn't turn out to be a bad night. I was actually in quite a good mood and was telling them some jokes which I'd got from Ricky, my boyfriend. Then Adrian was talking about drama school where he was at. And Dad was talking about vacancies at the factory and me getting a job there maybe. So, it was all OK. Dad told us some funny happenings which had happened to him and although we'd heard them a thousand times before, we all had a good laugh. I felt OK, in fact. Not bad at all. Two men came and chatted to Dad. Friends of his, and he bought them drinks. They stayed with us for a good half hour. I guess it went too quickly really. We hadn't arrived until late and the bell was soon going for last orders.

We left at about quarter past eleven and I felt happy. The evening had gone so well in the end and I'd enjoyed myself. So, I was feeling quite chuffed on our way home.

When we got back I helped Dad make hot drinks for us. But, would you believe that Adrian wanted to go to his room to study lines for a play he's in. At eleven-thirty at night! Dad talked him out of it, though and we were all in the lounge like a happy family. It was all OK until the subject turned round to Tracy and Tessa coming. Wow, that was something I didn't want to hear about. I tried to hang loose, though. Hang loose. Hell, what matters if they do come. Trying to hang loose when inside a fiery battle is raging. Like you're trying to keep control but all the functions are on resist. All the functions are on fight back for whatever its worth.

I'd never met them. Adrian had. He'd gone to the home to visit them. Dad had been visiting them for months, ever since they'd been in the home. Acting the good little Daddy and all that. I hadn't seen them, though. And I didn't particularly want to either. But, thinking about it, this time tomorrow they'd actually be here.

The tape Dad had put on had finished so I picked out a heavy metal one from my collection which I knew neither of them liked and when it started I turned it up really loud.

'Turn it down, Matti,' Ade said.

'Why?'

'I can't take it at this time of night. Some of us have been working all day, you know.'

Dad got up and turned it down.

I sighed and glared at his back.

'It's time you were in bed,' he spoke to me.

'Aren't we going to get the hard stuff out? Anyone got any smack?

'You can come and help me wash up,' Ade said. Like as if he would be stopping something from happening if he got me out. 'Come on. Collect the stuff.'

There was like a tension in the lounge. It was like they were watching me. Waiting to see what I would do. It didn't scare me, that atmosphere. I just sort of fed on it. Lapped it up like a cat drinking milk.

'You can do the washing up,' I retorted, 'On your own. I'm not running after men all the time.'

'Don't talk crap. You haven't lifted a finger for days. You do nothing.'

'Oh, Dad, he swore. I didn't think we were allowed to swear. You'll have to take his desk away. Then he'll have to learn to be good at something else.'

'At least I'll be successful at what I'm doing. I won't be a half bit musician, that's for sure.'

'Up yours brother.'

'Leave her alone, Adrian. You make it worse,' Dad intervened.

'It's about time someone filled her mouth in.'

I laughed. 'Such big words from a little boy.'

'OK, that's enough,' Dad said. 'Mattie, go up to bed. Without a word. Adrian, you can do the washing up.'

I just sat there. Looking down at my feet. Tapping them in time to the music. I suppose I was a bit nervous then. I remembered what Dad had said about me pushing him. Those words just came into my head. But it was like I couldn't take any notice of them. I was pushing him. Pushing him. Could I outsit him? Could I ignore his firm words. I was scared then. But it was like a fight. One huge, massive hell of a fight.

'Matti, I'll give you to the count of ten to get up to your room. Ten. OK? One . . . Two . . . Three.'

Sit. Sit. Sit. Spoilt bitch. You love him for Christ's sake. Why fight? Drum kit gone. Hi-fi gone.

I moved when he got to seven. I wasn't that damn spoilt. I moved quickly and left the room. What a bust up. Busting me up. He'd take my bed away if I let him.

I went up to my pad and shut the door.

Bucked out, kid. You bucked out. Yeah, but he's twice as big as me. And I've still got the taste of soap in

27

my mouth. I felt like playing my drums then. But picked up my guitar instead. Picked it up and started strumming. I turned my tape recorder on and began singing softly to a tune. I picked the strings with my spectrum. I sang for some time. Making up words as I went along. They were rubbishy words really. Didn't mean anything. Not to me. Not to anyone. I'm no good at anything apart from the drums. No good at anything. Absolutely nothing.

Chapter 7

I didn't get up until late the next day. Twelve o'clock to be precise. I made myself a cup of tea and then I just listened to my radio and lazed in bed. I didn't have much to get up for really. The big day, I thought. The big day. I dragged myself out of bed, washed and got changed.

Dad wasn't around when I got down. Ade was at college. I sat in the lounge and had some toast. Read the paper. I felt bored, you know. I didn't really know what to do with myself, so I decided to ring Ricky up. He was unemployed too. I thought, perhaps we could go for a ride out on his motorbike. I loved riding on his bike. And I thought, I've still got to tell the others about my drum kit. Not that I was really worried about that.

I rang Ricky and his mum got him out of bed to talk to me.

'Morning, yer lazy runt,' I greeted him.

'And you've been up since eight, I suppose.'

'Well, not exactly. What're yer doing?'

'When?'

'Today. Stupid.'

'Don't know. Haven't decided.'

'Shall we go out somewhere? You know, for a spin on the old machine.'

'Actually, I fancy going down the pub.'

'The others will be down there.'

'Yeah. That's the idea.'

'I don't fancy the others. Not today. Can't we go out somewhere alone?'

'Dad says you can have the hall today. If you want a practice.'

'You don't want to go out, do you? It's a nice day. You know, I thought.'

'Perhaps later.'

'Yeah. Sure. Are we going to the disco tonight?'

'If you want, yeah.'

'So, what we doing then?'

'I'll come and collect you. We'll go round the pub and see if we can get the others together for a quick session.'

'That's out for a start.'

'Why?'

'I haven't got any drums. We haven't got any drums. Anyway, hell, Ricky, no one's interested. We've had that out before. They're not serious about it.'

'What d'yer mean? You ain't got no drums?'

'I was a naughty girl and the stud took them away. He's given them to some kid.'

'Christ, that's great.'

'OK, so we go for a drink, then go out for a ride, yes?'

'Sure, OK. I'll be round in about half an hour.'

'Right, see yer then, bye.'

He was in the pub. Not Ricky. I went to the pub with Ricky. What is known as our local. Not Ricky was I talking about but him. Him with a capital H. He was in the pub. Standing at the bar. Leaning on it. Didn't my knees go weak. He was something. Real hunky dory. Sarah, one of my mates, started chatting to him. As if she knew him. I grabbed her as soon as I could get her on her own.

'Who's that blond hunk?'

'He's something, isn't he?'

'Who is he?'

'His name's Keith. He used to come to the youth club before he went away to university. He's back living with his dad now. He's into music too. Looking for a band or something.'

'Will you introduce me?'

'What about Ricky?'

'I'm not engaged like you. That's why I'm not. Because of guys like him.'

'I still prefer my Simon.'

'Oh, Sarah, you're so chronically in love. It's pathetic.'

'Where is Ricky?'

'Don't worry about him. He's playing pool. Just introduce me.'

'Sure. OK.'

We sauntered over to Keith and Sarah did the introductions. Wasn't he something. Especially when he smiled. He had hair which was gelled back and he was wearing a loose-fitting suit with a white scarf around his neck.

'Hello, Mattianna,' he said. 'Nice to meet you. That's an unusual name.'

'Her dad's Dave Kilroy. He's made a few records. Heard of him?'

'The name rings a bell.'

'Anyway, I'll leave you two to chat. See yer later, Matti.'

'Sure.'

'So, you've got a famous dad, have you?'

'Not quite.'

'I read a bit about him going into prison. I'm sure it was him. In a magazine. Going into prison for drugs or something. And then he turned to Christianity.'

'Yeah, he's got a big halo now.'

'That must be quite a change.'

'Yeah, sure.' I felt slightly niggled.

'I'm always impressed by people who have fought through something and come out on top.'

'Very impressive, I'm sure.'

'You're a very beautiful young lady. That must come from your mother.'

I smiled then. 'Well, it sure don't come from Dad.'

'I'm always jealous of people with fortitude because I haven't got any.'

'I wouldn't be jealous of him. He's made a bum of his life.'

'Bitterness doesn't suit you.'

I felt myself blush slightly and had a sip of my drink.

'You came in with someone?' he asked.

'Oh yeah. I'm meant to be going out with him, but I'm thinking of finishing it.'

'Easy come, easy go?'

'I need someone to stimulate me. He doesn't really. He's more of a friend.'

'I hear you've got a band.'

'If you can call it that. I'm thinking of pulling out of that. Starting afresh with someone else. The others aren't really interested enough, not really serious, like I am.'

'What d'you play?'

'I usually play the drums. But I sing as well. I guess in a way, I'd quite like to sing now.'

'I play bass. I thought of getting involved in a group now I'm out of university.'

'Really?'

'Yeah. I'm on the look out. People who are interested.'

'Are you serious.'

'Deadly. I want to be up in the lights. Kids screaming. Well, sort of,' he smiled.

I was quickly thinking. It didn't take me long to make up my mind.

'What about us starting a group? We'll need a drummer. I haven't got my drums any more.'

'I guess we could advertise.'

'Actually my brother can play the drums but I hate my brother.'

'So, we advertise, yes? Shall we sit down? Or would it be too much to ask of your friend?'

'Oh, he'll spend hours playing pool. Anyway, I've got to break the news to him sometime.'

'Said with not a trace of remorse. Are you like your dad?'

'Not a bit.'

'Of course not.'

I followed him to a table in an alcove by an open fireplace which didn't happen to be burning.

We sat down and were silent for a while.

'What did you study at university?' I asked.

'Law.'

'Really? D'you want to be a solicitor or something.'

'No. I want to join the police force.'

I laughed.

'What's funny, kiddo?'

'Nothing really. Sorry. I didn't know you went to university to join the police force.'

'I want to go in as a sergeant, higher up. With my degree I should be able to do that. Detective-Sergeant, that sounds good.'

'Detective?'

'Yeah. I want to go in on that side.'

'Plain clothes and all that?'

'That's right.'

'And you're serious about music?'

'One doesn't make it overnight. One might not make it. Anyway Dad insists I take a year off before I go in. He wants me to have gutsy jobs. Find out a bit more about the large old world. University life is a bit sheltered.'

'What does you Dad do?'

'Guess.'

'I don't know.'

'Actually, he's in the police force. Chief Inspector. It runs in the family. He is a bit eccentric, though. He does amateur dramatics in his spare time. Eccentric old boot he is. Solid though. You know. He's got a lot of wisdom behind his batty eyebrows.'

I looked down at my floating ice cubes. 'You love him, don't you?' I said.

'He's the only family I've got. I was their only son. Mum died six years ago. So the plucky old sod kept me going and his career too. I respect him for that. Yeah, and I love him.'

I looked into his eyes. There was a lot of emotion in them. A lot of something. I though I could understand and then I thought perhaps I couldn't.

'I'm sorry about your mum, Keith.'

'And I'm sorry about yours. Sarah told me. It's a hard old life, isn't it?'

'Yep.'

'Don't look so sad.'

'Oh, it's nothing.'

'I know it's nothing. It just won't go.'

'You understand that?'

'Don't torment yourself if you don't need to. You're right to chuck Ricky. He's no good for you. He hasn't seen anything. You know, he's immature.'

34

'Yeah.'

'You need a mature twenty-two-year-old, like me. How about us going to the pictures tonight?'

I looked at him. 'I was going to go to a disco.'

'With Ricky?'

'Yeah.'

'A film followed by a meal. Or a meal followed by a film, depending on what time you've got to be in.'

'Oh, any time.'

'You haven't asked yet.'

'I'll ask then.'

'You'll come?'

'I'll come.'

'Great. Give me your phone number and I'll give you a ring later on to sort out the times.'

'OK.' He handed me a piece of paper and pen and I wrote down my phone number.

'Well, I'm going to be off now. I'll leave you to deal with Ricky.' He winked at me.

'All right.'

He kissed me on the lips. Just ever so swiftly. Then he was gone. Out the door. Looking back once and winking at me again.

I sat transfixed for a while. Slightly dazed. I thought of Ricky. It had been on the wane for the past month on my part. Just someone to go out with. Nothing more really. Nothing more. Although I did feel a bit mean as I walked to the pool room with a single intention in mind.

Chapter 8

I walked home. Well, I had to really after chucking Ricky. I couldn't very well ask him to run me home. I felt guilty, though. Ricky had been so surprised and cut up. I also told him I was coming out of the band. I did feel guilty. I guess I wouldn't have chucked him if it hadn't of been for Keith. I wouldn't have chucked him. Still, Ricky will get over it. We weren't going anywhere particularly. Perhaps I'd used him. Perhaps I had and that's why I felt guilty. Still, it's done with now and there's Keith to think about. He's quite something, I thought, as I went in the back door. He's quite something. And we were going out that night. And he gave me a kiss. He must like me. At least he must like me. That made me happy. That made me so happy that I felt good to be at home. I wasn't even too bothered any more about today being the big day and all that. Well, I was still bothered. I suppose, I was. But I guess it just didn't seem so important. Funny how things can change.

'Afternoon, Matti.' Dad came into the kitchen where I was making a sandwich for lunch.

'Oh, hi.'

'Where've you been?'

'To the pub. I've chucked Ricky.'

He raised his eyebrows.

'I'm going out with a guy called Keith tonight. We're going to the pictures and then for a meal. It doesn't matter what time I get in, does it?'

36

'Get in by eleven and I won't grumble.'

'Eleven?'

'Em. I don't know this guy, do I?'

'But it's not as if I have to get up in the morning.'

'Films end ten-thirty. You'll be home by eleven. That will fit in nicely. Are you making sandwiches for me too?'

'No.'

'Thanks.'

'Oh, great.'

'There's some ham in the fridge.'

'O K,I'll make them.'

'Good girl. Who's this guy then?'

'He's just come out of university. He wants to go in the police force. His dad's a detective. He hasn't got a mother, either, so, I guess we've got something in common. He's O K. Interested in music. We're thinking of getting together. He seems O K.'

'Good. How did Ricky take it?'

'Oh, he was a bit shaky. He'll be O K.'

'Better to get out of it now.'

'Perhaps Keith will stimulate me,' I half smiled, trying not to look at Dad.

He ruffled my hair. 'You're learning,' he said. And it made me feel quite good. Perhaps it wouldn't be such a bad day, after all. Perhaps it wouldn't. Sod everything else. I suddenly felt quite happy. Quite elated, in fact.

I made the sandwiches and then a pot of coffee and took them in the lounge. Dad wasn't in there which was a pain. So, I had to go upstairs and find him. I heard sounds coming from one of the rooms, so went in there. It was for one of the kids. It was the first time I'd been in there. I knew Dad had decorated it. He'd decorated them both. But I hadn't bothered to see them before. I

37

knew they'd be tip-top. Well, I guessed they would. They were. I felt slightly strained at the modern, colourful decor. At the new furniture. I felt slightly strained, but pushed it away.

'Lunch is ready,' I said. 'A bit late at three o'clock. Aren't you having any dinner?'

'Not until about eight-thirty. We're not picking the girls up until eight.'

'Well, it's ready, OK? Dad?' He was bent over doing something inside a cupboard.

All of a sudden, as I was looking at him. As I was aware of the money which had been spent on the room. All of a sudden some words came into my mind. Blatantly. They pushed all other thoughts away. And they sort of mocked me.

You can't buy love. You can't buy love. You can't buy love.

The words took me unawares and sort of knocked the wind out of me. I turned and went out. Suddenly. It took me about five minutes to pull myself together. I did it locked in the bathroom. I sat on the side of the bath and felt sweat trickle under my hair, down my neck. Cracking up girl, I thought. Cracking up. Sure. So? You can't buy love. He can't do that. They won't love him. No, they won't love him. He can't buy them like he bought me. He can't do that. He's a Christian now. Christians don't do things like that. Buy love.

Funny. Ha ha. It's no good thinking. Not about things like that. It just makes yer feel weird. He didn't try to buy me, anyway. No. Yes. No. I loved him. Because. There was nothing else. Nothing else. It wasn't because I had everything. Because he was rich. I had him. Didn't I? Yeah, sure. I had my Dad.

I skipped down the stairs feeling OK. Went into the lounge where I sat on the beanbag and began my sandwiches. When Dad came down I reminded him that I wouldn't be needing a meal that night.

'Don't forget, I want you in by eleven. You can meet the girls then,' he said.

'Will they still be up?'

'Yeah. I've got a video they want to watch.'

Chapter 9

I was back by eleven. Well, at quarter to, Keith and I were sitting outside the house in his dad's car which he'd borrowed for the night. We'd had a great time. An Indian meal and then to the pictures to see *Top Gun*. It was really good. We got on, you know. I just felt so relaxed and happy with him. So at ease. I just enjoyed the night and had no thoughts of coming home to meet those two. I'd told Keith about them over our meal but, apart from that, I didn't think about what was in store.

It was only when we were sitting in the car that I thought about it and sighed. Surprisingly, I felt jittery. Nervous. On edge.

'What's wrong?' Keith asked.

'Because they're here, I s'pose.'

'Pinch of salt,' he tweeked my cheek.

'No, it's not. I've never even met them before. Everyone will be all over them. Especially Dad.'

'I'm interested. Carry on.'

I questioned him with a glance.

'You know. You're not happy about them coming. Scared? Jealous? Spill the beans, honey.'

'I don't know. Just feelings. I can't control myself sometimes. I just bring everything up. That's how Dad took my drum kit away. Because I couldn't control myself. You know, the lip and all that. Someone should cut my bleeding tongue off. I'm worried I'll mess it all up. I guess it's not their fault, is it?'

'No, I guess not. Does it have to be anyone's fault?'

I shrugged. 'If anyone's, it's his.'

'Why are you so bitter at him? You were the one he kept. You were telling me about all the good times you had with him.'

'It's all changed.'

'Yeah. OK.'

'Oh, I don't know. I was meant to have had him. I was the one with him. It doesn't make sense. No one knows. I idolized him. But he wasn't mine. He was never a real father. He just gave me bullshit. But I idolized him. Now, it's like he's throwing it all back in my face. He always told me I was his only daughter. That's when he was drunk. Although he used to write to the others he used to tell me that he didn't care about them. That he only cared about me. I believed him. Huh. I believed him.'

'Because you wanted to.'

'I never knew any other kids. I never went to school. Not for years. I just had tutors. I never knew anyone my age. Just friends of Dad. Some of Dad's girlfriends had kids but when I met them I just used to fight with them. It was crazy. I was lonely but I couldn't handle other kids.'

He didn't answer. Just stared out of the car. Deep in thought, he looked. Deep in thought.

'Oh, well. I guess you don't need my problems.'

'Of course I do. I want you to know I won't go spreading around what you say. It's just between you and me.' He touched my hand with his finger. 'You go in there and face it,' he said. 'I'll be thinking of you. I'll give you a call tomorrow night.'

'Thanks for the night, Keith. It was great.'

'Try to be good.' He cupped my face in his hands and then his lips came upon mine. We kissed. For a long

41

time we kissed and I didn't want it to stop. But he leant over me and opened my door.

'Remember, Matti.'

'What?'

'Bitterness doesn't suit you. Go on, get out. Be good. See yer.'

'Bye.'

I walked down our drive. God, I was more nervous than I ever thought I'd be. It was like stepping into the unknown. Not knowing what your own reactions were going to be to whatever would face you.

I waited a while before I rang on the front door bell. In fact, I counted to ten. It's a thing I do sometimes when I'm scared of doing something. I count to ten and then plunge straight in.

I rang the bell, heard the chimes and waited.

Dad answered and in a way I was glad he did.

'Hello, love,' he kissed me on the cheek. 'How did it go?'

'Fine.'

He took my jacket. I just stayed standing in the hall-way. Dad came, after hanging my jacket up and stood in front of me. He put his hands on my shoulders.

'I won't forget you,' he said and there were tears in his eyes. 'Come on in. They're looking forward to meet-ing you.'

I went in and I met them. My half-sisters. Dad's daughters who I'd never seen before. I went in and I met them.

Chapter 10

Lying in bed that night, listening to a tape of Simply Red, I thought back over the meeting. I guess it was kind of like a shock to see them in the flesh. Dad had introduced us and we'd all been polite. I'd been polite. Actually, I quite surpassed myself. Tracy and Tessa. Tracy was the eldest and looked the hardest of the two. Tessa, to be quite frank, looked terribly ill. Almost in pain.

I don't know how come I managed to keep control. Perhaps it was because I'd had a good night out with Keith. Maybe I didn't want Dad to be angry any more. Perhaps things were changing. I don't know. How can yer pick out reasons. It hurts. It still hurts. But there was something inside me on meeting them which persevered. So it actually, somehow, went okay. I guess yer could say it wasn't their fault. It was just circumstances, that was all. Just circumstances.

We'd stayed up until twelve-thirty. Having drinks and talking. Tracy was chatting away about the home and that she couldn't find a job after getting the sack from her first job since leaving school. Then she said she'd like to work in the factory if she could. And Dad said there was a good chance of her doing that. Along with me.

It all went OK. I felt pangs of hatred when they were laughing and joking with Dad. I realized Tessa really was ill when Adrian came in with a glass of water and some pills for her. I looked at Dad, questioning, and he gave me a glance which said he'd tell me later.

He did tell me later. He came into my room just a few minutes ago. Tessa has cancer. She's only been given six months to live.

I felt strangely sick hearing that news. Puky. A bit faint. As if I cared, though. I hadn't even wanted them to come into my life.

'Why didn't you tell me before?' I asked Dad.

He shrugged. 'You might not have taken the news well. You weren't too happy about them coming. I wasn't sure how you'd react. She's ill. We've got to give her more attention.'

'How come she's got cancer. I thought only old people got cancer.'

'No. Anyone can get cancer. Anything's possible in this world. Good and bad.'

I started crying then. Damn crap emotion spilling over again. Thoughts which just came upon me. Near on suffocating thoughts.

'It's something we've got to try and adjust ourselves to, Matti. She needs a lot of support at the moment. She's having some nasty treatment. It takes it out of her. She probably won't go back to the home. If we can manage with her, it'll be best for her to stay here.'

'Yeah. Dad?'

'Em.'

'I'm sorry, you know. About how I was. Oh, I don't know. It just seems so difficult, sometimes. Everything does.'

'I know. I know.'

'I didn't mean to be bolshie.'

'It won't be easy. I don't expect you to accept them just like that. Just try to be friends. They've had a lot of difficulties. It hasn't really been easy for any of you, I know that., It'll take time. Just think a bit before you react. You've done well tonight, though. Very well.'

'I like Keith.'

'Good.'

'We're going to get together music-wise too. He's all right, Dad. Quite intelligent too. Well, he must be to get a degree. I don't know what he wants me for. I'm only going to be a factory worker.'

'That's only a fraction of it. You've got to channel your talents out of work. Go for it, Matti. You've got talent. You've just got to channel all your energies in the right direction. It'll take time but you can get there.'

'Yeah. OK.'

'Right, goodnight. I'll see you in the morning.'

He kissed me on the lips and went out.

Chapter 11

The next few days. Well, it seemed as good as a honey-moon would seem. I s'pose it was hard in some respects. But we all seemed to cope pretty well. Tracy was friendly and we got on. Although, Dad told me, the crunch point would come with Tracy when she'd been living with us for a while. She'd get over the excitement of leaving the home and then the problems might start. I didn't really know what he meant. All I was interested in was the present and what was happening.

Dad fixed it for me and her to start work in the factory. Both on the production side. We were to start the following Monday which gave us just another week of freedom left. Funnily enough, Keith found a job to start the day after us. In a supermarket working in the bakery section. He was quite chuffed about it. We cele-brated by going out for a meal in this real flash place. It was great. Real romantic with candles at our table and everything.

It was weird, though. You know, somehow I felt as if I was on a cloud. Like in a bubble. I s'pose I did feel that I was in love. Keith and I really got on so well and we managed to find a hall for our music. Well, actually Keith's Dad had something to do with it. What with being a copper and that. In with everyone. He sort of wangled it for us and we could have it two nights a week for seven pound a session. Which wasn't too bad.

Anyway, I was telling Tessa about my music and what Keith and I were planning to do and that we were actually a bit stuck because we didn't have any drums. Because of what Dad had done.

'You know,' I said. 'I really feel uptight when I haven't played the drums for a long time. I really do. It's like it gets something out of me.'

'Why don't you ask if you can have them back?'

'He's sold them, hasn't he?'

She half smiled. I looked at her.

'He's sold them, Tessa.'

'Yeah. Of course.'

'Why are yer looking like that then?'

'I think he's just put them in store actually.'

'What? He hasn't sold them.'

'No.'

'Oh, bully for Dad. I wonder if I can get them back.'

'Matti?'

'What?'

'Didn't you want us to come?'

'Oh, sometimes I'm a pain, that's all. I go up and down, sort of.'

'You're like Trace. D'you know what she wants to be? Her secret ambition?'

'What?'

'An actress. She hasn't told anyone, though. She can be an awful pain at times too. Most of the time, in fact. Perhaps it's the home. I used to be a bit like her. Before I was ill.'

I looked down at my hands. It was kind of awkward, you know. Sometimes embarrassing, talking about her illness. She was in pain for a lot of the time. The pills helped. But the chemotherapy she was receiving made her sick a lot. It was horrible seeing her like that. I had to get over my awkwardness, though. Because I wanted her to talk if that was what she felt like. Talk.

'Oh, we used to have some laughs, though,' she said. 'Good times. Although it was never sort of stable. Always in trouble with the authorities. It's no good. She envies you, yer know. She always has done. You being with Dad. Inside she idolizes him. She never got on with our step-dad. Oh hell, what's the point, ay? What's the point of going on. I want to live. But sometimes it's so much hassle. So much hassle. I don't know if I'm going to live long. But sometimes I feel so tired. So tired.'

I took hold of her hand and squeezed it. 'You mustn't lose the will to live. Dad's going to get you in with someone else, isn't he? Someone privately who deals with cancer in a different way. I've been reading the book he's got. That cancer's caused by emotional things and if you can sort those out you get better. You mustn't lose the will to live, though. You mustn't, Tessa. You must fight.'

'I know. That's what Dad tells me. But I sometimes wonder what for. I always hated school and was hopeless at it. I'll just get a grotty job. If I was well I would. Then what? I don't want to get married. There just doesn't seem any point in it. Sometimes I wonder what living's all about.'

'Did you used to get on with your mum?'

'Oh, I used to write poems. All about a woman like her. She never understood kids. She was a snob, you know. You couldn't have a hair out of place or she'd jump down your throat. Our step-dad was strict. Really strict. It was crazy. He got me so wound up inside I used to be scared of men. I won't have anything to do with boys even now. I've never had a boyfriend. Oh, you know, I'm kind of neurotic, I suppose.'

'That makes two of us. So, we've got something in common. We can help each other.'

'I'm going to see this new doctor tomorrow. I'm scared really. It's alternative medicine, isn't it?'

'Yeah. And it's going to work. You're going to get better, Tessa. I want you to. It's all different now. You can stay here for good. It's all different. You need to get better. We're all fighting with you. You're not alone. You're never alone.'

Tears fell down her cheeks and I hugged her then. Hugged her so tight. How much I wanted her to get better. How much. More than anything. More than anything.

Chapter 12

I met Keith's dad the next day. He'd invited me round to dinner. I was right nervous and Keith was kidding on about it on our way there.

'He's an ogre really, you know,' he said. 'He eats little girls for dinner.'

'Not so much the little.'

'Very little. Impish like.'

'Piss off.'

'He hates girls using bad language. Really hates it. Don't slip while we're having dinner for Christ's sake. He'll never let you in the house again.'

'Keith! You're making it worse.'

He laughed. Loudly. Bellowing almost.

'Don't be a moron, Matti. He's a great old man. He's really looking forward to meeting you. Actually, he's got a proposition to make to us. He hasn't even told me, yet. Something to do with our music and his acting. I don't know exactly what his idea is. But that's one of the reasons he invited you round tonight.'

'What's it about?'

'I don't know. He's being very secretive. We'll have to see, won't we? He's really been preparing this meal all day. He's like an old woman.'

I smiled. 'But I hate meeting anyone new.'

'Lack of confidence that is. You'll be OK. At least you've only got to meet one parent. Of course, he might get called out half way through the meal. That's what usually happens.'

'The policeman's lot.'

'Pod the Plod.'

'What?'

'P the P. Pod the Plod. That's what I call him sometimes. Pod the Plod. Well, shortened to P.P. It's what I
read when I was a kid. A policeman called Pod the Plod.
I've called him that ever since.'

'Great.'

'Crazy really. He likes it, though. He's in touch with
teenagers, yer know. He understands them. He always
has done. I guess that's why I'm such a stable, sincere,
well-adjusted, handsome, eh, generous, intelligent . . .'

'Big headed. Conceited.'

'Hey, watch your tongue, young lady. You're ruining
my image.'

'And you're a poser.'

'I'm no poser.'

I laughed.

'A couple of minutes and we're there. Take your
valium now, Matti, or forever go in dread.'

'Do I look all right?'

'He'll fall in love with you.'

'Oh, really? Has he got much money. I mean would
he see me well off?'

'Very funny. We've got an agreement, my Dad and I.
Like contract. He keeps his hands off my girls and I
keep my hands off his.'

'Oh, your girls, ay? What about these girls?'

'Just a few, dear. Just a few. I am over twenty-one you
know.'

'Sure.'

'And you've had your guys. Which, I think is
absolutely disgusting. You being only sixteen.'

'Near on seventeen.'

'Even so.'

'OK, OK. We're odds on even.'

He turned into a driveway. In quite a smart road of semi-detached houses.

'All right?' he asked.

'I think so.'

'Come on, then. Let's go in and get it over with.'

Keith had a key and we went in an outer door to the front door which he unlocked. We went into a hallway with stairs leading off it and with a huge mirror on one wall. I quickly checked over my reflection to see if I looked OK and, although I say it myself, I didn't look too bad at all.

Keith called to his dad and took my jacket at the same time. Then this guy, tall, brown hair, brown eyes, came down the stairs. He looked smart in grey trousers and grey jumper.

'Hi, Keith. Hello, you must be Matti.'

'Yeah, hello.' I shook his hand.

'I'm really pleased to meet you. Keith can't stop talking about Matti.'

'Dad! How's the meal going?'

'It's going. Go into the lounge and give your lady friend a drink. I'll have the usual.'

'Sure, Scotch on the rocks. Come on, Matti. This way.'

'Don't go through the dining-room. I haven't quite finished.'

'Right, Dad. Through here, Mat.'

I thought the lounge to be rather old fashioned but stately. Neat for two men.

'What would you like to drink?'

'What've you got?'

'Most things.'

'Dry martini and lemonade.'

'OK, coming up. Sit down. Make yourself at home.'

'It smells nice anyway, the dinner.'

'He's not a bad cook, actually. Neither am I, come to that.'

'Oh, you're so modest.'

'Of course I am. That's the way to be. Here you are, madam. Aaah, would you like some ice?'

'If you've got some.'

'Yeah, we've got ice, no lemon though.'

He put ice in my drink and I took it, sitting on the couch. I felt better now that the introductions were over and I was actually in the house. His dad seemed friendly enough, anyway.

Keith took the drink out to his dad and then came back and put a record on. It was Bruce Springsteen, who I adore. He sat down next to me and chinked my glass with his.

'Well, it's not too horrendous, is it?'

'No.'

'Good,' he kissed me on the lips. Just a quick peck.

I felt warm inside. And I wasn't sure if it was the drink or his kiss. Or being there with him. In a house. Just me, him and his dad. In a way I was glad he didn't have any sisters or brothers. I liked it better that way. It made me feel sort of secure. Just the three of us was nice.

We both sat at the table in the dining-room when the meal was ready. It was a lovely setting. The table done with a floral centrepiece and candles at each end. Keith's dad served the food in a flurry. Joking as he was doing it. Quipping at Keith. It was all relaxed and we were soon tucking into the steak with a special sauce,

mushrooms, potatoes and peas. I was listening to Keith
and his dad chatting about this and that. Joining in when
I could. Then his dad told me to call him Mike and asked
me about my family so I told him about Tessa and Tracy. I
found I could talk easily with him. He didn't make me
feel on edge and he seemed interested. We were still
discussing it when he served the pudding which was a
choice of two different gateaux with cream.

It wasn't until we were having coffee that Mike started
talking about his amateur dramatics and Keith looked at
me then. We exchanged glances, both knowing that this
was the build up to whatever he wanted to suggest to us.
We waited, while he chatted on.

'Of course, what we're working on now, or what we're
going to be working on, is the biggest thing we've ever
done. It's big but we've got the talent. Some of the kids
are marvellous. RADA material. It's not the first musical
we've done but it's something special. It's something
new. To do with youth. We're putting it in for the county
competition. Well, we are. Of course, I keep trying to get
Keith involved,' Mike looked at me. 'Really, he should
mix the two, music and drama. He's got the talent. He
wants to go in the police force. Stupid sod.'

Keith sighed and did a mime of someone playing the
violin.

'Anyway, you're starting up a group. A band. That's
good. I think that's very good. What's better is that we
need a band for the musical. Like a rock band. All the
hard-core old stuff. You know it's going to be a bit on the
way back side. But we're in need of a band. So, I've told
my colleagues I think I've found a band.'

'Well,' Keith said. 'You've certainly got it roped up.'

'Obviously I wanted to get you two both together to
ask you formally. But, really, it's a chance you can't

miss. It'll get you a bit of publicity. Give you plenty of practice. And who knows where it might lead. We're not just a no-hope amateur group, Matti. Keith laughs us down but this could be our chance to make it. The winner of the competition gets the chance to play in London. And who knows what that might lead to.'

'He's a frustrated film star, that's his trouble,' Keith said. But I nudged him for saying that. In some ways I was quite taken by the idea. Yer know, if we could get a band together. Then why not air ourselves with a drama group?

'Well, I'd be quite interested,' I said. 'I mean, it would be practice and whatever way it goes there's nothing to lose.'

'What's this musical about anyway? Is it original?'

'We've got a free-lance journalist in our group. She wrote it. And some of the songs too. Although some of it will be well-known rock numbers. It's about two kids who leave home for different reasons. Go to the city. And they sort of work out all their problems through music.'

'That seems pretty way out,' Keith said.

'They get to know each other at this run-down disco and all their problems are somehow related with each other and to the music. Anyway you don't have to worry what it's about. You've just got to play the music. You don't even have to worry about a singer at the moment. Just get the music straight.'

'Well, I suppose it could be a good idea,' Keith finally admitted. 'What d'you think, Matti?'

'It sounds good to me. We'll have to get a band sorted pretty quick, though.'

'Yeah, well, we should get a response from the advert in the paper pretty soon. That's no hassle. We're going to need your drums, though.'

I sighed. I'd forgotten about my lack of drums.

'You'll have to get round your old man,' Mike said. 'I thought daughters had a knack of doing that with their old pas.'

'It's a good idea. Let's not think about the drums. It's a good idea.' And I truly meant it. There was a spark which was alight inside of me because of it. Something new. Something different. Just as long as I could get my drums back.

'So, what's your answer?' Mike said. 'Or, do you want longer to think about it?'

Keith looked at me again. Questioning. I looked at him. I couldn't say no. That spark was well and truly alight inside of me.

'I'm in,' I said.

'OK, Dad. We'll have a go.'

Mike reached out and shook Keith's hand. Then he did the same to me.

We talked a bit more about it, then moved into the lounge.

The rest of the night went so quickly. Listening to tapes. Laughing. Joking. Mike was telling me some police stories which Keith was fed up with because he'd heard them all before. But, all in all, it was a good night. Very, very good.

Chapter 13

Mike kissed me on the cheek when we said goodbye. He was great. I really liked him. My head was buzzing. With the night's happenings and the new venture. Keith and I didn't say much on the way home. Just listened to the radio. But we weren't sitting awkwardly. We were just both so happy. So happy. I don't really know why. We just were.

We stayed a long time in the car outside my place. We talked a bit about the evening but then just hugged, cuddled and kissed each other. I wanted to stay there all night with him.

'D'you ever think you won't go into the police force?' I asked, dreamily. Looking into his eyes which were so close to my own.

'The idea. It's got you going, hasn't it?'

'I just said.'

'Why d'you say it?'

'He said you've got talent. Haven't you got any faith in yourself?'

'My mother spent twenty years of her life writing book after book after book. Always dreaming one day one would get published. She finally gave up. A week later she died of a massive heart attack. She wasted twenty years of her life. Why? It nearly ruined their marriage. That's why Dad's into all this. Oh hell, I don't know. I want something more behind me, Matti. I don't want a dream which is nothing but a whisper in the dark. I don't want to go to my grave thinking I've failed.

It killed her. It killed her. Hey, you'd better go in.'

'I'm sorry, Keith.'

'Yeah, I know. You're my sweetheart and I like you a lot. Two more days of freedom. I'll ring you in the morning.'

We had another short kiss and then he opened the door. I got out and waited till he'd gone until I went in.

'How did it go?' Dad came out of the kitchen.

'I've got something to tell you.'

'D'you want a drink?'

'Yes. Chocolate please.'

I sat on one of the kitchen stools while Dad was making my drink and I began to tell him about Mike's idea. We stayed in the kitchen and Dad listened to it all. As I thought, he liked the idea. I guess that's all I needed, to know that Dad liked the idea, but I had a feeling there was something wrong with Dad. He seemed interested enough but sort of flat. His usual sparkle was missing. I didn't say anything about it, though. That's not until he changed the subject.

'I want you to do something for me, Matti.'

I looked at him.

'Go up and see Adrian. You two don't seem to have talked much for the last three days.'

It bugged me a bit. And like a fool I jumped.

'I thought brothers who were ten years older than their sisters were meant to be protective towards them. He's just an arrogant pain in the arse.'

'Yeah? And what are you?'

I was shocked at his tone. It was hard. I guess I still didn't take heed, though. The subject was too emotional for me.

'He hates me, Dad. He doesn't want me to talk to him.'

'Grow up, Matti. You're just jealous of him. Because

he is at RADA. And because he made it without me. And because he was mummy's boy. You're just jealous of him.'

'What's wrong with you? You've got the hump tonight, haven't you?'

'Well, that makes a change, doesn't it? From you having the hump.'

'Only I can't take your drum kit away, can I?'

'Watch it lady,' he pointed a finger at me.

I looked down into my drink. At the bubbles floating on it.

'He went for an audition today and he didn't make it. He's got an audition tomorrow for a TV serial and he's not feeling exactly confident. I thought if you went up and tried to buck him up, that's all. Give him a bit of support. He is your brother. He's had a lot to cope with as well as you.'

'He's old enough not to be living at home.'

'Well, you wouldn't know what it's like to be struggling to become an actor, would you? I'm asking you to forget about the hang-ups you've got and think about Adrian for a change.'

'Christ! What's the sudden surge for Adrian? The prize boy strikes again.'

'I'm not in the mood for your sarcasm.'

'You're in a mood, OK. Got the shakes?'.

I saw him coming but couldn't move out of the way in time from his hand which plummeted against my face. The force of it made the stool trip and me fall on the floor.

I just lay there a while, more scared than in pain. I was thinking, he's gone crazy. He's gone crazy.

'Get up.'

'Dad? What's up?' I heard Adrian's voice and felt pure relief.

'Make sure she's out of this kitchen before I come back.'

'Okay, Dad, take a walk. Forget it. Take a walk. I'll see to it.'

When I heard the back door open and shut I felt safe enough to move. I got up, picked the stool up and sat down.

'You shouldn't have tried him tonight, love.'

'Don't call me love like that. Anyway, what the hell's wrong with him?'

'D'you really want to know?'

'Oh, don't start getting at me, for Christ's sake. I've had a good night out, I come back here and nothing goes right. I'm sick of it.'

'I'm not getting at you, OK? I'm not getting at you. Don't jump down my damn throat. I didn't hit you.'

'No. What is wrong with him?'

'He asked Kathy to marry him. She said no. I don't know if that's the end. He wouldn't say.'

'Oh, sod.'

'Yeah. Quite.'

'Why did she say no?'

'Too many ties I s'pose.'

'Right.'

'Still, you weren't to know.'

'I'm sorry about the audition. That's what the argument was about. He wanted me to come and talk to you.'

'No. I wanted you to come and talk to me. We've all got to try and get on, Matti. Quit this arguing. It causes a bad atmosphere.'

'You're always the better one, though. Always the better one.'

'No, that's not true. I'm just trying to make a career.'

'Well, I ain't got one.'

'You've got to work for it. Don't poke at me all the time. I only lose my rag and we end up at square one. It's no good. Let's try again.'

'I had such a good night. Now, it's all ruined.'

'OK. If he's in a bad mood, he takes it out on you. I'll talk to him about it. He's had a hard day with Tessa as well.'

'How did she get on?'

'OK, for the first time. She's got to go twice a week. We don't know if it's going to work, though. We just don't know.'

'No. We never know anything. OK, I guess we could call it a truce. I s'pose it's my fault anyway.'

'Let's say fifty–fifty.' He reached out and took my hand. 'We'll work on it, yes?'

I nodded and had to hold back on the tears.

'Hey, this Keith guy seems OK.'

'Yeah, he is. So is his dad. I'd better go to bed, I s'pose, before he gets back.'

'Come on, then.'

Adrian came in my room with me and I actually told him about Mike's idea. He seemed keen on it. Said it would be good to get into. It was all right, you know. I got to thinking about that again and the spark came back. I've got my life to lead. As Dad once told me. I've got my life to lead.

Chapter 14

I hated Sunday night. The thought of going to work the next day. I was starting at eight-thirty in the factory. Great, it was just fantastic. To be quite frank I could have done without it. I nearly told Dad I wasn't going. But he was going round as if he had a great weight upon his shoulders so I decided I couldn't actually tell him I'd changed my mind about work.

Anyway, Keith came round and we were up in my pad. Talking. He was looking forward to starting work. I don't know why. I must be a lazy cow. But, it's not really that. It's like starting work is admitting defeat. You know, admitting you haven't made it. So you have to go to work. To earn a living.

I was plucking my guitar. Right grumpy. Keith was sitting in my rocker reading a magazine.

'Christ, Matti. It's not that bad,' he said.

'It is.'

'We've got to start work on the band.'

'We won't have the time, though, will we? We won't have the time if we have to work.'

'It's the big old world. You have to get out there. Go for it. You really have. It's no good otherwise. That's what living's all about.'

'OK OK.'

'Yer Dad's taking you, isn't he?'

'Yep.'

'That's OK then.'

'Oh, God, I'm just so pissed off. I mean it's not

exactly going to be exciting is it?'

'Have you composed anything just lately?'

'No.'

'Well, do so. It'll buck you up.'

'I can't do anything without my drums. That bastard won't give them back to me. What's the bloody point?'

'Maybe, if you talk to him. You know he hasn't sold them. Get Adrian to talk to him.'

'I just feel so uptight.'

'Frustrated?'

'I don't know.'

'Let's make love.'

'Very funny. I don't think I could make it.'

There was a knock on the door then and Tessa came in.

'Hello, Tessa,' Keith said.

'Hi.'

'Come in and join the happy throng. D'you want to lie on the bed?' I asked.

'No. I'll sit on it.'

'OK. Are you all right?'

'Yeah. The pills help. I've just taken a couple.'

'Sorry. I look at you in pain. And I feel guilty at being fed up.'

'Why're you fed up?'

'She doesn't want to start work and she's missing her drums.'

'Tracy will be there.'

'Yeah.'

'Let's put a real, hit with it, beaty, tape on,' Keith said. 'What yer got Matti?'

'I don't want to listen to anything.'

'Oh Christ, you are bad.'

'I just want my drums. I can't compose without my drums.'

'You should have thought about that before you gave him lip.'

'Oh, very funny. I didn't know he'd take my drums.'

'Well now you do.'

'Sure, now I do.'

I lay back on my beanbag and stared up at the ceiling. It wasn't right. Nothing was right. It seemed to be one cock up after another in my life. I couldn't get anything straight. Nothing straight at all. Just the thought of my drums. The feel of the wood in my hands. The sound of the beat. Oh, if I ever thought I wanted to play the guitar. I wanted to sing lead instead of playing the drums. If I ever thought that, then I apologize to myself. I was wrong. I needed my drums. For my own sanity. I needed my drums.

I was just lying there. Feeling perfectly no OK. No dreams. No hopes. Blank. All blank. I was bugged. Bugged good and proper. When Keith motioned to me I thought he was just mucking about. But then he started pointing to Tessa. So I looked at her. She was crying. Sure, she was crying real tears. My heart suddenly went out to her. Sure, I felt bad. For all my own selfish thoughts.

'Tessa?' I got up. Went over to my bed. 'Tessa? What's wrong?'

'It's OK. It's OK. I'll be all right.'

'Look, Matti, I'll make a move, OK? I'll give you a ring tomorrow night. I'll let myself out.'

'OK.'

Keith kissed me on the cheek but I hardly felt it. I sat on the bed beside Tessa and wrapped an arm around her. She cried for a while. Really heavily.

'Tell me, Tessa. Talk.'

'You don't want me here, do you? That's why Kathy

wouldn't marry him. Because of us. Me and Trace. Dad
hates us now. He does. He just pretends.'

'Oh Christ, Tessa, you can't mean that.'

'I do. I do. He thinks he can take us back, but he can't.
He never wanted us. He never did. You don't want us.
Your drum kit and that. It was my fault.'

'Oh, Tessa, Tessa. You've got to be kidding.'

'He's been so down these last few days. He loved her.
He needed her to marry him. He's got no one. What can
we give him?'

'Forget it, OK? Forget it. He's just being bummish,
that's all. He does love you, Tessa. He does. He's a hard
man to understand. He's trying, though.'

'He hit you.'

'Yeah, that was nothing.'

'Sometimes I wish he'd hit me.'

'Why?'

'Because I can't cope with him being gentle. I'm not
used to that. This bloke I talked to. He was saying
things. Asking me questions about my step-dad. Well, I
just kind of shut up. I didn't say anything. But I can't
cope with being in a family where they love each other.
I'm dying but I want so much before I die. I don't think
there's enough time any more. I'm running out of time
and I'm so scared. I want it all now. But I'm so twisted
inside. So twisted, I can't cope.'

'Tessa, listen. If you want something badly enough,
you can get it. You can. If you want to live badly enough
you'll live. I'll never give up on you. Those damn doc-
tors with their chemotherapy. Have faith in this alternative medicine. Have faith in it.'

'I don't mind dying as long as I die happy. But I'm so
screwed up.'

'OK. So we unscrew you.'

She half smiled, through her tears.

'No. I'm not kidding. We'll make it. We've got all the time in the world. I'll help you, Tessa. You've got to get it all out. Get it all out.'

'I've got to love again.'

'Yeah. So?'

'So, I'm not sure if I can. So much pain. Hatred. Bitterness. That's what eroded me. Nothing in this house makes me sad, Matti. It's all within, though. All within. I'm full of filth.'

'You're full of genius. That can come out. For everyone's benefit. Those poems you showed me were great. We can work on something.'

'I had a dream the other night. And there was like a halo of light. All around a stage. And there were people on that stage. They were sad for some reason but they were happy to be doing what they were doing. It was you. I'm sure it was you and Keith. You were there, leading it all. You've got to work, Matti. But the light will be on you one day. I'll be watching too. Wherever I am.'

'You're not going to die, Tessa.'

'I guess if I ever get ready, God might take me back.'

'Oh, shit.' I was crying then. Crying. How could I feel such love for a sister whom I hardly knew. How could I? I was burning up inside. I felt her hand on my hand.

'You've made me happier by talking.' I can't talk to Trace. I guess she's got her own hang-ups.'

'So have I.'

'But I guess, through it all, Dad was a wise teacher. You're self-sufficient. You can cope alone. I guess you've had to. I'm going to bed, Matti. Tell Dad when you go down.'

'I love you, Tessa.'

'Will you go to work tomorrow?'

'Yeah.'

'Right. I'm going to bed.'

'D'you need any help?'

'No. Just let Dad know.'

'Yeah.'

I watched her walk slowly out. God, she had something. She had some sort of power. I could almost feel it vibrating around the room. I could never think of her dying. I could never think of that. But sometimes the way she spoke sounded like an old person talking. An old granny. Close to death. No. No. I can't think of her dying. But I lay on my bed and cried. I cried. Because somehow there was a part of my heart which could almost see her going to a God I didn't believe in.

Chapter 15

I'd kept out of Dad's way ever since he'd hit me. We'd only spoken a few words to each other. Passed each other by when we happened to meet. I guess I needed him just then, though. I felt scared and lonely, so scared and lonely. Lying there, in the dark. Trying not to cry about Tessa. Trying not to think about my drums.

I went downstairs and into the lounge. Dad and Adrian were in there playing chess. I poured myself a lemonade and sat on the sofa. Neither of them said anything. Oh great, I thought, lovely to be noticed. Huh, that's men for you. That's men.

'Dad.'

He looked up at me and smiled.

'Are you OK?' I asked.

'Come here and watch this checkmate,' he patted the side of his chair.

I went over there. It was his move. He was really thinking it out. He'd taken loads of Adrian's pieces. I could play chess myself but wasn't very good at it. Dad was brilliant, though. It was checkmate the next move.

'What's that then, Ade? The score?' Dad rubbed his hands together.

'Four–two. You lead.'

'Four–two, which will be the score on Saturday. In Arsenal's favour, of course.'

'How much are you going to put on it?'

'Tenner.'

'I'll make it fifteen Spurs will take it.'

'On.'

They shook on it.

'That's how I earn my bread,' Adrian spoke to me, winking.

'You haven't got the money to throw about. You should curb your gambling habits, son. You should curb them.'

Adrian packed the chess pieces away.

'Keith gone?' Dad asked.

'Yeah. Tessa came in. She was crying.'

'Was she?'

'Yeah. She's gone to bed now.'

'What was wrong?'

'Well, you should know.'

'Why should I know?'

I shrugged. 'She thinks she's going to die. She's got a lot of problems. She wants to get them sorted before she dies. But she doesn't think she's got the time. And you've been so bolshie. I know why, but you have been. Will you talk to her?'

'Yeah, I'll talk to her.'

'Thanks.'

'When are you and Keith getting the band together, then?'

'We're going in the hall on Thursday and a couple of guys are coming to audition.'

'It's all happening. You're auditioning again on Thursday aren't you, Adrian?'

'Yep.'

'Will you find out then if you've been accepted?' I asked.

'Should do.'

I looked down at my fingers. I guess I wanted to be pleased for him, if he got the part. It would be his first big break. It was hard, though. I so much wished it was me.

'He's worked for it,' Dad said as he was taking me and Tracy home from work on Thursday. He'd told us Adrian had got the part in a new television serial. Actually, I'd heard half way through the day at work. Natalia had come down to the factory to tell me. I guess I was happy. It was just the thought that everybody would be over him. He wins again, I thought. He wins again.

'He's worked for it, Matti. He's twenty-six. Well time for a break.'

I was sitting in the front of the Mercedes. Dad was wearing a yellow jacket and sunglasses. Looking the real, cool part.

'How did work go, Trace?' He looked in the mirror. Tracy was sitting in the back.

'All right. I'm still fitting those rubber valves, but Guiseppe said I might move on tomorrow. Matti's moved on already.'

'Happy, Mat?'

'Yeah, it's all right.'

Work was all right, much to my amazement. It was a small factory. Small, clean and airy, with clean tables to work on. There were about twenty people in all, working there. Some young, some a bit older. Guiseppe was in charge of us. He was an Italian and he was all right. He kept winking at me anyway. The factory makes ball valves. So we have to assemble the valves in a small, metal frame. That's what I've been moved to. It's all right. I've been moved to a table with an older woman called Maggie, a black girl, Debbie, and another Italian, a woman of twenty-four. I got on well with them. They were all friendly. We chatted a bit while we worked. There was also a radio on all day which came across the tannoy which meant we had something to listen to. So, all in all, it wasn't as boring or as bad as I first thought it would be. Actually, you know, you could get quite a rhythm going on the valves. What with going in time to the music. I was reaching quite a speed. I had races with Debbie because she was the fastest. I could keep up with her on about two frames but then I'd cock it up and she just sailed right on. No, it wasn't bad. Three days working there and I almost felt as if I'd settled. Course, there was Dad who came down to the factory floor from the office quite a bit. It got round somehow that he was our Dad. It made me feel sort of chuffed. Great. You know, it chuffed me in one way but then in another I thought I was letting Dad down by just working in the factory. I guess, I must be a snob or something. Roll on tonight, I'd thought, half-way through the day. Roll on tonight and the audition for the band. And I'd be seeing Keith again. The audition wouldn't take long and then Keith and I would be together. Alone. And we could make music alone and sometimes when we did that – him playing the guitar and me singing love songs – well it was really great. Really sort of soppy. And we'd be alone in the hall so goodness knows what would happen. Goodness knows what would happen.

Chapter 16

When Dad suggested that Tessa come along to watch the auditions I nearly died. I really did. It was damn crazy. We couldn't be alone, Keith and I, if Tessa was there. We couldn't do anything. Hell knows it would be just like being at home. I couldn't just turn round and say no, though. I had to say yes, didn't I? Just had to say yes. But it really bugged me. It was over dinner and after I'd said yes I just sort of had to stop myself from snapping at everything Dad and Adrian said.

I went upstairs after the meal and lay on my bed. Who was I kidding, anyway? That it would be a great night. Who was I kidding? What could I do without any drums? But, it wasn't that. It was really just to be alone with Keith. That's what I'd wanted and now Dad had completely spoilt that. Was I bugged or was I bugged.

When there was a knock on the door I half yelled to answer it. Tracy came in.

'Hi,' she said.

'Hi.'

'What's wrong with you?'

'Nothing.'

'You could have said no.'

'What yer talking about?'

'You don't have to act like a saint just because she's got cancer.'

'Look, forget it, OK?'

'What was the plan? You and Keith make love to the music?'

72

'Piss off.'

'She should get out of course. She will enjoy it. She likes you. So, don't feel too bad about it. Your good deed for the day.'

'What d'you want, Tracy?'

'A fag.'

'I haven't got any.'

'Right, well, have a good time with Keith tonight, then. I'll tell Tessa she'll be the gooseberry.'

'Don't be stupid,' I got off the bed and went after her. 'Don't you dare, Tracy.'

'She's not that fragile, you know.'

'I don't mind if she comes tonight, OK?'

Tracy shrugged and she gave me a look which I could have slapped her round the face for. I didn't though. I slammed my door instead and punched my pillow.

Why us, I thought. Why cancer? Like mum. Like mum. Like mum. Coming back. Again. Striking. Why? God knows, I don't. I don't. I felt so screwed up. I really needed to play my drums but the hell I couldn't. And then Dad shouted up that Keith was on the phone for me. Which did lighten me just a bit. Just a bit. But I didn't feel in the mood for any full-blooded romantic conversation.

He sensed my mood as soon as I spoke.

'Something wrong?' he asked.

'No.'

'Is it Tessa?'

'Oh, just life. Tessa's coming down to watch the auditions. Do you mind?'

'No, of course not.'

That annoyed me slightly, that he sounded so blasé about it. As if he'd had no idea of wanting me and him to be together, alone. Like I had. Like I had. It doesn't matter. Nothing matters. Let's be in a good mood to my boyfriend. What of it if our ideas don't run even.

'What d'you want?' I asked.

'Ever thought of your Dad making a comeback. Getting back in a band?'

'Oh, yeah.' Who's twiddled your bow, I thought. 'He thinks about it sometimes,' I said.

'Ask him if he wants to come for an audition.'

'Pull the other one, Keith.'

'Well, it would be a start. For him. For us.'

'He's forty-nine, for Christ's sake.'

'Oh, come on. He's still got talent. Dad and I were listening to one of his old records. In fact Dad's going to ring him.'

'Keith, have you gone nuts! This is our band. For the musical. Young people. Dad's old country stuff.'

'We could get him back on the road again. You can play the drums. Haven't you ever talked about it to him?'

'Let's change the subject.'

'It's a right-on idea.'

'Climbing on his back, you mean,' I half mumbled.

'I heard that.'

'Well, it's true.'

'I don't have to climb on anyone's back. Neither do you. You know that. Just a gentle comeback, that's all. Talk to him, Matti. Tell him to come down tonight.'

'A right family affair. Don't you ever think of anything else?'

'I'm not quite as bitter as you.'

'That was a bit bloody snide, wasn't it?'

'How you're feeling. OK, I'll see you tonight. At eight. Down the hall. With or without your Dad.'

'OK. See yer, bye.' I practically slammed the phone

74

down. Just sat there for a while. Why does family have to come into it? Dad playing in our band? Dad? OK. So maybe it was a good idea. But it was all for slimy publicity, that's what it was all for. Slimy, cheap-skate publicity. I'm not using my Dad for anything. Not for anything. Who cares anyway? I get sick of family. And just thinking that, I thought of Tessa and knew it was wrong of me to think that about family. And I felt so screwed up again. Thinking, why the hell can't I get rid of this screwed up feeling of tension inside me.

'I'm only thinking of you, Matti.' Keith rang back, didn't he. Keith rang me straight back while I was just sitting by the phone. 'I mean, it might be a bit of publicity for us. But, you know, your dad did get somewhere. People would be interested. Father and daughter in the same band.'

'For this musical thing?'

'They're a top drama group, Matti. Some of them are at RADA. This competition. With the right band, they'll sail it. And there's something. It would fit in better with the story if there was someone older singing vocals. Dad and I were talking about it and we just sort of hit on the idea with your Dad. That's all. It would only have to be a one-off thing. Just for the musical.'

'Well, OK, maybe you're right. Maybe I'll say something. I don't know where he is at the moment. He's just popped out with Adrian.'

'All right then, well keep yer pecker up and I'll see you later. Everything's going to shine, babe. See yer later.'

'OK. Keith?'

'Em?'

'Sorry, you know. I guess it's a bit Tessa.'

'Yeah, I know. Don't worry, OK. See you, darling.' He blew a kiss down the line and I did the same before putting the phone down.

Chapter 17

It was all right. I had Keith. It didn't matter about anything else. Surely, it didn't matter about anything else. Anyway, Tessa's going to be OK. Dying? The thought hadn't crossed my mind. It's just the strain, that's all. And I don't really know what I think about Dad being in the band. I guess it's a good idea in one way. For him. For us. Maybe it's a good idea. But somehow it was like pressure. Pressure which I just wanted to get away from. Get away from it all. Just like that.

It has changed. It has definitely changed. But I've coped. I'm not jealous of Tessa and Tracy. How can I possibly be jealous of Tessa, anyway? How can I? They've fitted into the family. And it hasn't been bad. So, why do I feel so strained inside? Like wanting to do something but not knowing what. I'd been OK at home. Not getting at Dad. Not getting at Adrian. Everything so perfect, I thought. As I sat fiddling with the phone. Everything's so damn perfect. Happy family and all that. It angered me. I felt anger biting at my very gut. I had to move. So I got up and went into the lounge. Tessa was in there. She hadn't looked quite so pale just lately. Not so pale. If I knew she was in there I wouldn't have gone in the lounge. But she smiled and, once there, I couldn't just walk out again. So, I had to sit down. Bugged, though. Real bugged. But I couldn't let it show, could I? I couldn't let it show. It was all wrong anyway. I had to be prepared to give Tessa everything. Not feel bugged. Not feel bugged.

'How're you feeling?' I asked her.

'Nervous about going to that doctor again.'

'Oh, it'll be all right.'

'It's like the past happening all over again.'

'Yeah, I guess it is.'

'Dad understands. I guess I'm lucky because he helps me through it.'

Stab. Stab. Stab.

Get the knives out God and stick them in me, why don't you? Why don't you?

'A lot of it's about anger,' Tessa continued. 'It's like some people let the anger out. But some people just can't let it out and it turns inward. That might cause cancer. Well, that's what he reckons. So, it's like going back through everything that's made me angry. But it's like I don't really want to remember. He forces me to. So does Dad. I guess that's the best thing really. I'm talking more now, though. To everyone here, more than I ever have done before.'

'Yeah.' Talk. Talk. Talk. And I couldn't fight back. I couldn't hit Tessa. I sort of half smiled at that thought. I couldn't hit Tessa because she might be dying. You really shouldn't hit someone when they're down.

'Are you OK?' she asked.

'Fine.'

'Sure?'

'Yeah, I'm all right.' Nothing's wrong with me. After all, I haven't got cancer, have I?

'I'm looking forward to coming with you tonight. I wonder if they'll be any good?'

'Hope so.'

'And the musical and that. It's a really good idea.'

'Yeah.'

'You're not very talkative tonight.'

'I'm all right.' I half snapped.

'How's work?'

'OK.'

'D'you want a cup of coffee?'

'No. I'll make you one, though.'

'I can make it. I'm not a cripple.'

She was crying when she went out. She always damn well cries. To make the coffee was an excuse for her to get out. But I could see she was crying. Why the hell did she always have to cry? It drove me crazy. It really did. Because it was like it was all my fault. All my fault.

I usually ran after her when she cried. I could usually help her a bit, but then I was past helping any more. I really was. I just had to get out. Hit the air. Find some space.

I went through to the kitchen and practically barged out the back door. Not looking at Tessa. At her tears. Not wanting to see it, any more. I walked round to the back of the house and through the gate which led to the fields and river.

I told him, I thought. I told him it would all change and it has. That's why I had those parties and that's why he took my drum kit away. That's why. Because I knew it would happen. And I'd be left out in the cold. Yes, I knew it. So why did I apologize to Dad for being so bolshie? I had a goddamn reason to be bolshie, because I knew what would happen. I knew it and I was right. Dad can't love everyone. All his attention on them. Now Tracy's the bolshie one and she gives him lip. Now Tessa's got cancer and everything has to stop for her.

Where does that leave me, Mr his man in the sky? Where does that leave Matti Kilroy? I'd like to know. I'd like to damn well know. I kicked at a large log. I kicked at it again and again.

I'm not going to cry, I thought. I'm going to be strong. Perhaps I will leave home. Make my own life. Find other people to love me. Even Keith's all over him. Even Keith is. Big Dad. Big talented Dad. Everyone's running after you like they've always run after you. Nothing will ever change. Nothing can damn well change, can it?

Why do I want to be in a band, anyway? Following in Dad's footsteps. Why? What's so special about being in a band? Who cares? It'll all end up the same anyway. With me being left out in the cold. That's what Dad wants. I remind him too much of the past, I guess. I bet he'd like me to leave home. So, perhaps I just will. Go travelling. Just to forget the whole lot. Even Keith. Love? I don't know anything about love and that's the truth. I don't know anything about it. Because I've never been taught. Daddy's never taught me. Daddy's never taught me.

I sat on a lump of grass and threw stones into the river. I wanted to cry but forced myself not to. Tessa's the only one who's got any right to cry round here. Tessa is. Tessa. Tessa. Tessa.

'Shit,' I half shouted. 'Shit.'

It's no good swearing. No. Good little girls mustn't swear. Good little girls must always be good little girls and then perhaps nothing will ever change. Nothing. If I'd been a good girl, perhaps if I'd believed in God and gone to church, like I should have done if I was a good little girl, I would never have had those parties ruining the house. I would never have been bolshie to Dad. Never.

Huh! And so I will be a bad girl and I won't win then either. But perhaps it is right. Perhaps I shall win after all if I am a good girl. Perhaps I shall grow up. Be really mature and take this full in the face like a woman would take it. Perhaps then there won't be so many hard feelings. So many heartaches. Perhaps.

Then I shall pray, instead of throwing stones into the river, I shall pray. Just like this. Even if I start crying. I guess God doesn't mind if I cry. He's not going to say, God I'm fed up with you crying, like I say, God I'm fed up with Tessa crying. And it makes me all annoyed. All annoyed. Just like that. God won't say that or think that of me because although I don't know God, I really don't think he would be like that.

So, I just sat there and spoke alone to God, whom I'd never spoken to before. I spoke alone to him so there was just him and me and no one else.

'Dear God Father. The Father of my father. That's what he thinks, anyway. How can yer lead a man? Him. To destroy me. It's all crazy. Everything is going on. Everything is going on and there is such a rush inside me. Such a rush which I need to escape from. A darkness. You are meant to have given the light. That's what you are meant to have done. Made the world. Made me. Me? Huh, that's a laugh. Have a classic laugh on me, God. Have a classic laugh on me. Oh, hell knows. I do wrong, I s'pose. In your eyes I do wrong. And if you believe in your almighty power, you should always do right. You should always do right. You know what puts me off you, God. You know what makes me really want to kick you in the teeth. Christians who think they've got you taped. That they know what you want for everyone else. Like they will come up to someone and say, I really think you're not doing God's will. They think they're so goddamn perfect. Someone once told me I couldn't be a true Christian until I knew seven verses of the Bible by heart. And she was such a cold looking woman. She didn't have an ounce of warmth inside her. If you're there you're there for love. That's what I believe. To love us and we should love as well. I do think that's the most important thing. But hell, that sort of people really stops me praying and stops me going to church because I can't see any love inside them, any love at all. And they're the ones who pretend they want to save people. Every other word of theirs is Praise the Lord. Praise the Lord. Think of it, Mr God, that really makes the Lord seem so pathetic and alienated from the world. Praise the Lord crap. If I believe in Jesus I will never say Praise the Lord. I will praise him. Yes I will, but sure as hell, in a different way to that. That just drives people away and it sure does make me want to vomit sometimes when I think about it. So this is me, God. Talking to you about why I don't believe and what stops me. Because sometimes, I want to believe, I really do. Then I think of stupid cretins who think they're perfect and different from everyone else and all they can see is how you're not doing something right and it's all meant to be in the name of the Lord. Its just as well Dad doesn't go in for all that rubbish. He does believe in you, though, and he does believe in Jesus. And that fact just makes me think sometimes. Which really isn't what I was meant to be talking to you about. But I just wanted to air my views so you'd know first-hand how people like me feel. It's like certain people are pushed away. Pushed away from you. I can see it and it makes me angry, although I have never talked to you before about it. Besides anger works in different ways. Sometimes I feel so angry inside. Sometimes I need more support than I'm getting. Sometimes I seem to need so much and I feel so weak and useless. So weak and decrepit. Like a little worm buried underground. I don't even really know what I'm meant to be doing with my life. There's my drums. Sure, there's my drums. Where's the fire, though? And what about this musical? I don't know, sometimes I just feel like I'm being carried on and that I haven't grown up and I want to be different. I guess I just wanted to copy Dad by being in a band. But success isn't everything, I know that. Success isn't everything. Dad ended up on drugs and in jail because of success. In a way I guess I used to be proud of that. But maybe I'm not any more. Maybe I'm not.'

I stopped talking and looked into the river where a black fish kept jumping out of the water and flipping this way and that. So free, I thought. So free. And then I thought of Tessa. Of her having cancer. Perhaps there is an answer. Perhaps there is an answer in that fish. So free, fish. So free. I wished Tessa was a fish. I don't want her to be in any pain. But why should I care. Sister? I couldn't think of that. A secret perhaps. Still think of Tessa. That is all I'm worried about at the moment. And then jealousy still bites, like the fish will bite the bait. And there is something I have to learn. Something I have to find out. About me? Maybe. About the world?

'I don't know anything, Mr God. I don't know anything. That is the blatant fact. Nothing to make me grow.'

But there is the fish and he knows nothing either. And there is the bird in the tree and he knows nothing. But they are beautiful and they are free. And I guess God looks after them. I guess he does. They don't know how to save Tessa. Like I don't know how to save Tessa. And perhaps they don't know how to control their feelings, like I don't know how to control my feelings. So perhaps, just perhaps, I can be free and able to control my emotions and nothing will hassle me any more. Nothing will hassle me. And there was like a stream of water inside me then. A stream of water which was calm and which had the sun shining on it, warming it. And there were trees circling the stream. They were full of greenery. Then I suddenly felt inspired and I didn't want anything to spoil it. I didn't want anything to ever spoil it.

I made a decision as I walked back. I made a decision. I didn't want to be in the band. Not that band. Not in the musical. I didn't want that. I don't know why I made that decision. I just did. Just then. It doesn't matter about me not having my drum set any more. Why was I so excited about Mike's idea? About the musical. It was all so different then, though. Like a different me. Perhaps a change *had* taken place. Although all I know of it is that I don't want anything to do with the band any more. It's different, I guess. Playing on your own in your bedroom. It's different to being in a band. And I have to make a decision about my life.

I understand now. I understand now something which I've never understood before. But it is so deep inside me, that understanding, that I can hardly claim to hear it. Or to listen. It's just there and I know. I know. I have other gifts which I can find and which can be used. And that will make me into a woman. Not a silly little girl. I can grow and I can cope with Tessa. Even if she dies. Even if she dies. Then I know something good would have happened. I will have that assurance within. That assurance which Dad has now and which I can't quite understand. That time. That place. Striving for something. A battle within. I have knowledge. Some knowledge because I am sixteen and I have lived sixteen years. And now I want to be wise too. Like mum was wise. Yeah she was wise.

I went in the back door and just stood a while in the kitchen and then Dad came in.

'Where've you been, love? I've been looking for you. Ten minutes we're going down the hall.'

'You are. I'm not.'

'What?'

'I said, you are. I've changed my mind. I don't want to get involved in it.'

He stood, looking mildly flabbergasted. 'What d'you mean, Matti? Look, if it's the drums.'

'It's not the drums. It's not anything. Just me making a decision.'

'I'm not having anything to do with your band, Matti. I know what ideas are spinning round but I've made my point clear. I'm not getting involved, you don't have to . . .'

'Christ!' I butted in. 'Can't I even make a decision? Can't I? I mean, am I still a five-year-old unable to make up my own mind? Why does there have to be a reason? I've just made up my mind. I'm not a kid any more, Dad. I don't need to be told what to do. I don't. That's the truth. I'm out of Mike's idea. I'm out. I don't want it. You go with Tessa. I'll let Keith know. I'm going upstairs.'

He let me go. He left me alone. So I went upstairs. Into my room. I saw my drums, back in their place and for a while I just stood there looking at them.

'Why the hell is it so difficult?' I spoke to no one. I spoke. I didn't want to get near my drums but I was drawn to them like a magnet. I sat at them and picked up the sticks. I thought of Keith and then I thought of Tessa. When my door opened I didn't look up.

'Can I come in?' It was Tessa.

'You're in.'

She came in and she sat on my bed. She wasn't crying.

'I'm sorry,' she said.

'Yep? What's that meant to do? Make me feel guilty?'

'It wasn't meant for that.'

'No, OK.'

'Are you going to play the drums?'

I didn't answer. Took the drum sticks and began tapping. Rolling my drums. Roll. Roll. Roll. And there was so much energy coming from somewhere that I switched my tape on and began drumming to the music. It was so brilliant. So damn brilliant. All the power in the world was in my possession. All the power. And nothing else mattered. Nothing else mattered.

So I played the drums to the music as Tessa was sitting there and in a way I was praying my own prayer by playing the drums. I was doing that. I played until sweat dripped down my face. I smiled when I stopped playing. I smiled. This is it, I thought, this is really it.

Tessa said nothing. She watched as Dad came in, though. And I followed her gaze to Dad. Standing there. So in control. That's funny. I've realized, the only time I'm in control is when I'm playing the drums. That is the only time.

Dad smiled at me.

'Are you two ready to go?' he asked.

I nodded. 'Don't we need the drums, then?'

'Keith's done some tapes for the auditions.'

'OK.'

'Right, Tessa?'

'Yeah.'

'Come on then.'

As I was going out of the door Dad said, 'I'll never take your drums away again, Matti.'

I looked at him.

'You need them. Because you're dedicated. You're really talented. I have faith in you. Never think of giving up again. Never let it cross your mind, because you're going places.' Then he kissed me on the forehead and ruffled my hair.

This must be you, Mr God, I thought as I walked down the stairs. This must be completely you. Because I am that stream again with the sun shining on it. And I am the young tree with roots. My food. Give me always my food and I need not worry about growing any more. I need not worry about that. And maybe I need not worry about Tessa either. Maybe. Maybe. Maybe.

Chapter 18

It turned out to be one fantastic night – although in three hours Keith and I just had about fifteen minutes of privacy, where we could be alone together. And that was all right too. In fact it was more than perfect. That made the evening although it had already been made really. Firstly the two guys we auditioned were A OK. One was a guitarist and one was a saxophonist. We got together almost straightaway and did we all click but did we all click. It was just as if we'd been playing together for years. And that was without me on the drums, that was just with me singing. But I felt so keyed up with it all. I just wished we'd brought the drums down. But the rhythm and the sound. I could practically feel the way I would play my drums and how it would fit in.

Mike was there and one of his friends from the drama group came too and there was like a buzz of excitement going round from everybody. Mike had brought some music and we were playing old rock and roll numbers, Beatles' numbers and a couple of songs that the guy had written himself. You know it was funny. Although I used to play in the other band, it just didn't measure up to the feeling I got second time round. This was something like on fire. Pulse rate. It made your old adrenalin go. And everyone was so happy. Even Tessa spent half the night tapping her feet and laughing along with us. Rod and Dave, the other two guys were great. So friendly and cool. Really with it. As I said before we all just sort of clicked. And in the end it turned into an all-out practice session instead of just an audition.

I was amazed how well Mike and Dad got on. And then Dad had to get up on stage. He couldn't hold out any longer. And it was really something hearing him sing again. Really something special.

'You've got to be in,' Dave, who had short hair which stood up on top, half yelled. After a couple of numbers with Dad. We'd all been talking about Dad and music before so they knew the score. I must admit I was so high I had to agree with him.

'Just right for the part. Just right. You've got that look about you,' Mike's friend said.

'I'm an old man now.' Dad tried to put them off but I could tell he'd really enjoyed being on stage again.

'We won't find anyone better,' Mike said.

'What d'you think Matti?' Dad turned and looked at me.

'Well, he did give you your drums back,' Keith quipped.

'I don't mind if you're in,' I said. Meaning it too. With the whole of my heart.

'Just for the musical then,' he said. And we all cheered because it was that kind of atmosphere. It was like someone had touched the whole place with magic.

'Just for the musical.' He wagged his finger at everyone in sight, but I'm sure I saw a tear of happiness in his eye. He was just so glad to be singing again. I knew that. And it made me feel good too.

'OK what about a Johnny Cash one then, Dave Kilroy. Johnny Cash one. That's what we want. Isn't it boys and girls?' Mike pranced around in front of the stage as if he was some kid.

'OK, let's do it. Got one here. "Walk the Line,"' said Rod.

'All right. Come on Matti. Be my partner. Let's find the words.'

While Dad was finding the words, Keith whispered in my ear after giving me a quick peck. He whispered in my ear, 'Because you're mine I'll walk the line. Bit old. Not with it. But from me to you. Love is just perfect. From me to you.'

'Hey, stop canoodling you two,' Mike pointed a finger at us.

'Jealousy will get you nowhere, father.'

'All right, we got it. After three.'

So we sang and played and laughed and had a great night. So that everything seemed perfect. So that Keith and I went outside, leaving the others to do the clearing, and sat on a small seat in the garden.

'How d'you feel?' he asked. Wrapping an arm around me.

'High.'

'I know you do.'

'Don't you?'

'Yeah, I feel high. It's strange, I felt it was what I was really meant to be doing.'

'Perhaps it is.'

'I don't want to argue any more. I don't want to feel bad. I just want life to carry me along. Like that. A ride of a leaf. When are we going to make love, Matti?'

I giggled.

'D'you want to?'

'Yes. I don't want it to be for no reason though.'

'Like I love you reason?'

'Yes.'

'Do you love me?'

I looked into his eyes and squeezed his hand. But I said nothing.

'OK. I'll accept that. It takes time.'

'I do love you. I do.'

'I won't push you either way, OK?'

And then we just kissed each other. A real tongue-pushing kiss and Keith touched my breasts and I felt so warm. So exhilarated. Yes, I thought. Yes, I want to make love to you. I really do.

When we got home I went straight upstairs to play my drums. Remembering the music we played and trying to find the rhythms. Counting the beats in different ways. I was so intent that it made me jump when I suddenly saw Dad standing there. I hadn't heard him come in.

'Oh Dad, hi.'

'Hi. That sounded all right.'

'I was just packing up.'

'You were far from packing up. Call it a day, though. Tessa's just gone to bed.'

'OK.' I put my drum sticks down and climbed from the stool.

'Thanks, Dad. For the drums.'

'You're on a trial period, OK?'

'Yeah. OK.'

'Coming down for a drink?'

'Are you in a good mood?'

'What?'

'I remember what happened the last time you made me a drink. How's it with Kathy?'

'Hey, the last time I made you a drink, you gave me lip, OK? Button it, lady.'

'You were grouchy, though.'

'I'm entitled to be sometimes aren't I? I'm no saint.'

'Don't they teach you that at church?' I half smiled.

'Hey, I'll have you.' He raised a hand to me but it was only in a joke.

'Sorry, Dad. How did it go with Kath?' I asked as we were going downstairs.

'Let's say things are looking up.'

'Is it because of us, why she didn't want to get married?'

'No, it's not that.'

'Are you sure?'

'Why? What're you all going to do? Bugger off.'

'Sure. If that's what you want.'

He stopped on the stairs and looked at me. 'Many a true word is spoken in jest, you know that?'

'Yeah.'

'So?'

'It's your life. Why d'you need us hanging around?'

'I'm your father and I love you. It's about time I showed it, isn't that right?'

I looked down at his fat belly.

'Maybe it's too much of a sacrifice,' I said. Quietly.

'No. My joy is seeing you happy. All of you. My joy will be seeing you be able to cope in the big, wide world. Any sacrifice will be worth that.'

'You love Kathy, though.'

'Yeah, but if it's not meant to be, it's not meant to be. You were right, I was grouchy. I apologize, Matti. But you survived. That's what life's about. Surviving. Come on, let's go make that drink.'

We made that drink. Tracy joined us and Adrian was already in the lounge. We watched telly for a bit but then switched it off. They were talking. I was just content to listen. I suddenly felt safe. Very safe. Dad wanted us. He wanted us. So much so that he would be prepared to sacrifice Kathy. That was unheard of. In all my life with him he'd always put his woman first. He'd changed now. Yes, he'd changed and I'd thought it was for the worst. But at times like this, perhaps it was for the better. Perhaps it was. I felt safe. Happy. I had Keith. Keith who inspired me. Made me tingle. It hadn't been like that with Ricky. Ricky couldn't stretch himself. So, just then I felt happy. Nothing seemed bad. Absolutely nothing. I felt as if I could reach for the sky and touch a star. Go for it and all that.

'Hey.'

I was suddenly woken from my dreams by a piece of rolled up paper which hit me on the face. I looked at Dad, where it had come from.

'Stop dreaming of sex and lust,' he said. 'I don't want you corrupting that new boyfriend of yours.'

'I wasn't dreaming of sex and lust. Why d'you always think the worst? I'm not like you, yer know.'

Tracy laughed.

'You should clobber her for that,' Ade said.

'I wouldn't clobber her, would I, darling?' he looked at me.

'I'm going to bed.'

'She's getting out of that one.' Ade smirked 'Goodnight, Matti. Sweet dreams.'

'And they won't be full of sex and lust either,' I threw the piece of paper back at Dad.

'Aren't I getting a kiss goodnight, baby?'

'Seeing as he gave you your drums back.'

'OK, seeing that. I might consider it.' I went over to him and gave him a quick peck on the cheek.

'Goodnight, love. God bless.'

'Goodnight all.'

Chapter 19

I don't know what made me first wake. There was nothing definite. It was three-thirty, so I turned over and was going to go back to sleep again. That's when I heard Dad and Adrian talking. Urgency. Nightmare. Tessa's name. Lights were on outside my room. There was movement. I was suddenly startled. I heard something else. Something else. Like a groan. Tessa. Panic. I jumped out of bed. Went out my door and along the corridor. Ade was in his room. Getting changed.

'Ade?'

'Oh, Matti. It's all right. We've got to get Tessa to hospital. I've phoned the ambulance. It's all right, the doctor's been and Dad's with her.'

'What's happened?'

'I don't know. She's in pain. Very weak. I don't know. We've just got to get her to hospital.'

'Oh, Christ.' A panic filled me. I wandered along to Tessa's room and pushed open the door. I didn't want to see her. I didn't want to see her being ill. I didn't want her to be in pain. I felt sick. Faint. But I still walked in her room. Over to the bed. Dad turned and looked at me but didn't say anything. Tessa was moaning. She looked deathly white. She looked at me but it was as if she didn't recognize me. All a con, I thought. All a con. She's not dying. She can't be dying.

'D'you want to sit with her for a bit?' Dad asked. 'Just hold her hand.'

I sat where Dad had been sitting. Took hold of her

hand which felt so cold and limp. Dad went out. It was just me and her. I wiped her forehead with the flannel.

'Tessa, it's Matti,' I said. 'It's Matti. It's all right. You're going to be all right.'

It was as if she was trying to speak but no sound would come. Her eyes met mine then, though, and this time they didn't seem so vacant.

'You'll soon be in hospital,' I said. 'Just keep on going. Keep fighting, Tessa. You're going to be fine.'

'Pain.' I caught her word. Pain.

'I know. I know.' I squeezed her hand. 'I know. But it will soon be better. They'll give you something. Then you can rest. The ambulance will soon be here. You'll get a free ride, ay?' I tried smiling.

Tears started to roll down her cheeks. God, what could I do? I felt so hopeless. If I could magic her pain away. If I was Jesus Christ himself and could heal her pain by some God-given power. But I was hopeless. Ever heard of the word futile? This is what it means. Nothing else. Just this.

Dad came in and took over after a little while. He said the ambulance had arrived and he was going with her while Ade was to follow later in the car. I kept out of the way when the ambulance men came in. I went down and sat in the kitchen. Completely numbed. In shock.

It didn't take long for the men to get her out and off. Dad quickly got his coat on and went with them. It was terrible. I didn't want to think of Tessa but that was all that was in my mind. Tessa. Tessa. Tessa. All the time.

'All right, Matti?' Adrian came in.

'Is she going to be all right?'

'Let's make a cup of tea.'

'Is she going to be all right?'

'I don't know,' he half snapped.

'What about the new treatment? I thought that was meant to work.'

'Miracles don't happen to us, do they?'

'I just want her to be well.'

'We all do.'

'It just feels like a part of yourself, that's what. You can't do anything.'

Adrian put the kettle on and prepared the tea. He sat opposite me and looked down at his hands.

'I don't know if she's going to make it, Matti. I don't know how strong she is.' Tears came down his face.

'She's got to make it. I hate it. I hate cancer. Why does God let it happen? She hasn't done anything to anybody. Nothing's her fault. She doesn't even smoke.'

'No. I know.'

'What're we meant to do now?'

'Have a cup of tea. Go to bed. Try to get some sleep. She's in the best place now.'

'But she was so happy tonight. Seemed so much better. How could she suddenly get so bad?'

He shrugged.

'I won't be able to sleep. I'm going to wait up until Dad comes home.'

'You should try to sleep.'

'I won't be able to.'

'Lie on the hammock.'

'Yeah.' I pushed my tea across the table and went in the lounge. I turned the small spotlight on and lay on the hammock. A pain deep inside me. I prayed. I prayed because there was nothing else I could do. It was beyond me. Completely beyond anything I'd ever felt before.

I did go to sleep. There on the hammock. I woke at six o'clock. Wondering for a moment what I was doing on the hammock. Then I remembered. I remembered and I cursed myself for falling asleep. In a strange way it was like I'd betrayed Tessa by sleeping. I went into the kitchen and the new morning's light was filtering through the curtains. I made myself a cup of coffee and sat drinking it. It was seven when Adrian came down.

I looked at him. Needing to know. Desperate to know. He put his hand on my head.

'She's comfortable. She's all right. They had to give her a blood transfusion. But she's as well as can be expected.'

'Why did it happen?'

'It's spreading, Matti. It is spreading.'

'Oh, great.'

'I don't think they can do much. Just ease the pain a bit.'

'So, she's going to die?'

'We mustn't give up. This new treatment. The doctor's going to see her. Dad got in contact with him. He's going to see her today.'

'Yeah, but it's too late, isn't it? It's too damn late. It should have happened years ago. This new doctor. It should have happened years ago.' I stood up and tipped my coffee down the sink. An anger filling me. An anger at life. An anger at the world. People. People who didn't care. People who were just out for themselves. People have problems and no one cares. Hate. Bitterness. Hate. Envy. Greed. This is it. This is the way it's going. The world. The people.

'Morning all.'

I swung round at the sound of Dad's voice. Temper biting at my gut.

'Why are you so happy? She's not ill now, you know. She was ill before. Who cared? You left her. You've come too late, Dad. You've come too damn late,' I yelled at him and then barged out of the kitchen. Up to my room. Slamming all the doors I had to pass through.

I sat on the drumstool and picked up the sticks. I turned the tape on. Just habit. An automatic reaction. Then I let loose on the drums. Let loose on them. Feeling so frustrated. So angry. Tears coming. But I kept pounding on my drums. Wanting to be lifted away from my feelings. From my heart. Just lift me away. Lift her away but lift me away too. Do it. Do it. Because I can't stand this. I can't stand it being so unfair. So very very unfair.

Chapter 20

It was awful having to go to work. Awful. I didn't want to do anything. But I went. There was something inside, though. Pushing me on. Pushing me on. To some limits. To some outrageous limits. I just wanted to stay at home and play my drums. But determination seemed to churn through all my veins. Churning up. Keep going. Tread on.

I worked hard. Able to keep up with Debbie. Guiseppe commented upon my work. He praised me for working so hard. Asked me if I was all right. So did Maggie when we were both in the loo. I told her. I told her. And then later Guiseppe called me outside.

'I've heard about your sister,' he said. 'I'm sorry. I'm sorry. Keep yer chin up, ay?'

I nodded. 'Yeah.'

'If you feel upset just take a walk, OK? I don't mind.'

'I'll be all right.'

He prodded me in the stomach and I went back to my workplace.

So, someone cares. What a laugh. So someone cares. Bitterness erodes. Bitterness erodes. Inside. When it's not even acknowledged as bitterness. Just a lack of hope. Lack of faith. Futile. Nothing's futile apart from the end.

'I want to talk to you,' I spoke to Dad. When we'd arrived home. After dinner. When he was clearing up.

'Fire away,' he said.

'No, not here. Let's go for a walk, shall we?'

'Leave the washing up,' Adrian said. 'I'll do it if you want to go now.'

'All right, ta, Ade. Get yer jacket then, Matti.'

We walked all across the fields at the back of the house and to the river where I'd been sitting the other day. It was a warm evening although not sunny. We sat on a different fallen tree from the one I'd sat on before. I had to pluck up the courage to talk to Dad about the things I wanted to speak about. It's all right thinking about it alone and wondering. But to actually bring it into the open is a different matter. Is a different matter entirely.

'OK, love. Get if off your chest.'

'Well, it's just like I've been thinking.'

'Em?'

'You know, thinking about like why you go to church and things. I don't know, I've just been thinking.'

'Why I go to church?'

'I mean, how come? Why did you change. What's it all about? You never believed in God before. I think, Tessa and that. It's just a feeling I've got that she has faith. It shows. Something special in her shows. I don't know what. If I knew I was dying I'd be scared. Of what was going to happen. I mean I've got no faith. I've never thought about it. Is there a God? Isn't there a God? Now, I'm just wondering, that's all.'

'There's got to be an answer, you mean?'

'I want to ask and find the answer.'

'It's not that simple. You believe in God and you believe in Jesus and things aren't that easy.'

'How come you believed? You changed.'

'I met this guy in prison. The rector there. I guess I was feeling the same way as you are now. I was at my lowest in prison, though. Down. Really down. I even thought about taking my own life. It got that bad. So I just went along to the chapel one day and sat there. I was there two hours before he came and sat down next to me. He had some power. He really had power. I talked about my life. The parties. The drink. The drugs. I told him all about it and then he asked me about my childhood and I just broke down. I cried, Matti. For the first time in years, I cried and he comforted me as if I was a child. Then he prayed for me. We prayed. I felt something, Matti. I felt some sort of power as I was down on my knees. Me? Can you imagine? Down on my knees. No, not *the* Dave Kilroy. Not the big he-man having to admit someone was greater than him. It was a fight to get down on my knees but once there a calmness came over me. A peace. I'd never found that before. Never. Never. It had to be something. I went back to my cell. Cried again, but didn't feel so desperate. There was something there. I wanted it. I needed it. Jesus Christ. Yes, nothing fantastic happened. I didn't change overnight. But I made a promise to myself that night that I'd believe in Jesus. That I'd give him a chance. Just a chance. I went back to the rector the next day and he taught me. I saw him for the rest of my time there. He taught me about true wisdom. How to love others. How to endure. Yes, that was the reason I changed. But I'd reached the pits, Matti. The pits. He brought me out. He really showed me the right way.'

I listened and took it in. There must be something in it, I thought. There must be something in it. But half of it seemed unreal. As if it couldn't touch me. Although, in a way I wanted it to. Although I wanted to feel something. Enlightenment. Perhaps I was after some enlightenment.

'Why does God make people so ill? Suffer. You know. What about all the suffering? Tessa hasn't done anything bad.'

'I can't give you the answer, Matti. Faith isn't clearcut. There is no answer. It's something within which is an assurance of faith. If we had all the answers there wouldn't be any need for faith, would there?'

'Is Tessa scared of dying?'

'No, I don't think she is.'

'I don't want to lose her, Dad. I don't want to lose her.'

'Pray for her, Matti. Pray for her. Pray for you. Have faith. Believe in Jesus. Believe in him with your whole heart. He believes in you. He'll be with you. Believe in him. It doesn't mean you have to go and be a nun. Just find him quietly by yourself. He can show you the way to go. He needs you as much as you need him. He loves you. He loves you.'

I don't know why I felt arsey then. It just came upon me. Right real grumpy, I felt all of a sudden. Right real grumpy. I turned away from him. And anger mounting in me but an anger which I wasn't sure of.

'What's wrong, Matti?'

'I don't know.'

'It's a fight, isn't it?'

'Come on, let's go home.'

'You can't run from your feelings, Matti. Let them come. Be aware of them.'

'Yeah, OK. I'm meant to do no wrong and all that. If Jesus is so great why is the world like it is?'

'Because there are not enough people with true faith. They're all content to do little things. It's the big things that matter. Now it is. It's the big things.'

'Yeah. So? OK, let's go home.'

I began walking away. I didn't want to talk any more. I didn't want to feel any more. It all seemed too much. Perhaps one day earlier I would have just mocked Dad, but somehow it had got beyond that. Something was happening inside me. Like some sort of a threat and it was because Tessa was dying and I didn't want to lose her. That was all. If I could cope with that I'd be OK. I didn't need God. I didn't need Jesus. I could make it on my own. With my own assurance.

Dad and I walked back in silence. I guess he thought there wasn't any point in saying anything else to me. Whatever, he kept silent and I was glad.

Chapter 21

I went to see Tessa the next evening. Adrian said he'd take me after Dad and I got in. I'd bought her a couple of magazines and some chocolates. Adrian told me Keith had rung and I suddenly felt guilty because I hadn't rung him before.

I rang, before we left for the hospital. I told him everything and he was very sympathetic and understanding. I told him the ward she was in and he said he'd send her a card. It was nice hearing him. It was like he brought a bit of sanity back to me. Sanity to save me from religion. I must have been crazy even thinking of such things. Low. Reach the pits. Like Dad did and you turn to amazing visions. Self-illusion. Self-illusion, that's all it was. I had to try and convince myself anyway. I just had to.

Tessa was in her own private room. She was propped up in bed and although her eyes were sunken and dark and her face was still a puky colour she seemed to have more life in her than the last time I had seen her. She seemed much brighter. She smiled at Ade and I when we went in, and we both hugged and kissed her before pulling up chairs and sitting down by the side of her bed.

We talked about this and that. Nothing definite. Little things. The weather. The hospital. My job. Adrian's acting. It was weird though. It was almost as if we were consciously skirting around what we wanted to talk about. Not that I really knew what it was. It was something to do with Tessa and I, though. It didn't involve

Adrian. Perhaps he knew that because after we'd been there about half an hour he said he was going for a walk to let us get on with woman's talk. I thought that was very noble of him.

'I'll be back later,' he said, before kissing Tessa and leaving us. When he'd gone Tessa sighed and smiled at me.

'Has the pain gone?' I asked her.

'Mostly.'

'Good.'

'Tracy was in this afternoon. They let her take the time off work.'

'Yeah, I know.'

'I wanted to see her. She's all right, you know. She is all right.'

'Tessa.'

'Yes.'

'What is there to say?'

'I did some writing. I want you to read it. I want you to read it.'

'Where is it?'

'Under my pillow at home. It's in the notepad. You know, it's about everything. Everything.'

'You will write some more, Tessa.'

'It explains things. I think I have found peace now.'

'Don't give up.'

'You accept, rather than give up.'

'Are you scared?'

'No.'

'How come?'

'Mum's waiting for me. I want to be with her and granny. I want to be with them. You will be a success, Matti. I know you will be.'

'You can't die.'

'I always needed Dad and I've found him now. Perhaps that's all I needed. Parents are important, you know. They are important. I guess that's why everything in the world has gone so bad. Because parents don't realize how important they are.'

'I know what you mean.'

'I guess you missed your mother.'

'Yeah.'

'Now she's watching and waiting but if you don't know that, it must be hard.'

'I want to know it.'

'You'll find out one day.'

'Will it be too late?'

She smiled. 'No. No. Go on. You've got life. That's very, very precious.'

'Tessa?'

She reached out and took my hand.

'Tessa, I need you.'

'I need you too. Please don't cry for me.'

'Sorry, I can't help it. Sometimes, I'm so scared. Of what's before me. So scared. I don't feel whole. I don't feel complete. I'm scared I'll be left alone without anyone. You've got so much faith, Tessa. So much faith. I envy you for it.'

'No. Everything has its time. Believe in Jesus and there is no end. It's not very difficult. Not when you're dying. It'll be more of a fight for you than for me.'

'Yeah,' I wiped my eyes. 'I'll read what you've written, Tessa. We'll use it.'

'I might be coming home in a couple of days. I don't want to stay in here. I want to be in my room at the end, with my family.'

I nodded.

'So, we'll talk again, won't we?'

'Yeah, of course.'

So, that's how we ended our conversation. What was needing and waiting to be said. It came out. And then Adrian came back in and I went for a walk to let them have time together. I walked down the long, brick corridor. Doors leading to wards on either side of me. It was bleak. Death was in the air. I walked and felt deflated. As if I was a burst balloon with no air left inside me. What matters if I've got spots, for goodness sake? I've got life. What matters if I've got bad breath? I've got health. I'm not dying. What matters about it all? Why should I feel lost? Beaten. Why worry? Nothing's futile. Life's what you make it. Life's what you make it. If you're breathing you should go for it. Anything. The sublime. The ridiculous. Climb the highest mountain. Swim the stormiest sea. Don't be oppressed by the system. Don't be put down. Just go for it. I will, Tessa. You've got nothing. You're dying. I'll go for it. Scared? Why am I scared? Nothing should scare me. Believe in God and you'll go places. Little things don't matter. It's the big things which matter. It's the big things which count. Now it is. Now.

I believe in you, God, but people can go to hell. The people who run this country. Oppress the poor. Put in prison those who are afflicted. Why do you kill? Why do you die? Evil. Against good. It's a battlefield. I can see it. It's a battlefield. Then I shall put on my amour and go to battle. Yes, I feel power. I shall go forward. I believe I'm unique. I'm special. I'm God's child. Nothing to do with religion. Just between God and me. Jesus and me. I belong to them. That's all. Deep in my heart, that's all. Simple. And I felt some sort of a peace as I walked back to Tessa's ward and room. I felt some sort of fucking peace.

Chapter 22

It was weird reading what Tessa had written. Pages and pages. Her feelings. Her torments. Her hopes. It seemed they had all flowed out of her. Like water from a turned-on tap. I could feel her pain. Feel her anguish. Always searching. Always searching for something which seemed beyond her. She loved her mum, that was evident. She loved her mum and she watched the woman she loved being torn apart by a brute. A callous, evil, brute. It was that more than anything else which made her have faith.

> I see evil [she'd written]. I see the very depths of Satan. If there's evil then there must be something else. An opposite. There must be good and good must come from someone. Some being. Somewhere in the universe. There must be someone to conquer evilness. I always have hope. I've found hope in my prayer. There is a voice which says go on. Which says there will be a day of peace. No matter what roads one has to walk upon. I must walk towards that peace. Walk on, although I can't understand. There are no answers. No answers. The desperate cling to straws. Then I am desperate. So much hatred. Frustration. When I tell Mum I hate her, I don't mean it. I think she knows. Perhaps she doesn't. I dream of the day my real father comes and rescues her from her torment. He's my hero. The invisible hero. He rejected me but I have faith.

Perhaps I can understand why he only writes twice a year. Perhaps I can understand why. It's hard. Very hard. The desperate cling to straws. I guess he's my straw. I guess he is.

My faith in God isn't strong. I see churches in my mind but I don't want to go. The world should be different if the churches really worked for the mighty. I don't believe in religion. I want to fight on my own. I want it to be between God and me. He's there, I know he's there. Especially now I'm ill. I feel bad. I'm ill. The tablets the doctor gives me help. But I still feel bad. I have to go for tests. What will they find? I'm not worried. I'm not worried.

That section ended. She'd left a page and written some more. Like in a poem.

> Strangers,
> Always strangers,
> In my house,
> Not knowing them,
> I feel so apart,
> So apart,
> Because of the cancer,
> In my body.
>
> What do they feel like
> When they hate so much?
> What does Tracy feel like
> When she steals from shops?
> Another disease,
> Like cancer,
> Only this one kills.
>
> My life ahead,
> Shortened,

So much to see,
So much to hear,
To feel.
All gone.
Dreams,
No point,
Schemes.

I tell Mum I love her,
Tracy, I can't reach,
But they're all strangers.
I need my Dad,
He'll sort it out,
Don't make me die yet,
Don't make my life end.
Pleading,
Pleading,
Please don't.

Hopes. Visions. Cascades of froth. Froth of gunge. Clear now, clear now. He's come. Mum had to die, but he's come. Touched by an enigma. Touched by a force. We go out. I talk. We go out. I laugh. It's what I've always wanted. He's the father I've always needed. Wisdom. Wisdom. Words. His. I'm at peace. Scared. Scared of dying but he makes it seem so natural. Wait for me, he says, wait for me.

'Again,' I say.

'Sorry. There will be a time.'

'Yes, I believe you.' I believe him. I believe him. There will be a time. Oh, for heroes. They make everything safe. The make everyone safe. No heroes, no sanity. No sanity. No security. Then you get Tracy. You get rape and you get violence. I

know. I know because it either turns inward or
outward. With me it turned inward. God help me.
It turned inward.

I put her notepad down and lay on my bed. In a
strange kind of way I felt ashamed. Because, in a way,
I thought I was the only one to ever go through any
pain. Any torment. It was like the number one in the
world was me. No one else. I mean, had I ever realized
that other people suffer too? Had I ever realized that?

I felt ashamed and angry at the same time. Because,
just because. Angry, because she was my kid sister.
The kid sister I'd never known. Angry because of that,
and because as my kid sister she was put through so
much anguish. And she had no one. Not then. No one
who really understood her. There go the rest, I
thought. All of them out there who are struggling on
alone. And it is not only I. It is not only number one
herself. So you have thousands of kids who feel
they're unloved. Thousands who dream of their own
hero. Searching. Searching. Finding. And finding. Perhaps. Who's the lucky one? Who's the lucky one out
there? Put your hand up and count to ten. How does it
go? Kiss my arse. Anger. Yes. Who understands why
kids fight? Who needs excuses? No one needs those.
Just the knowledge. Just the wisdom. You don't need
excuses. Just heroes.

Who was her hero? Dad was her hero. Dad. The
father who always has to be the hero. It sure don't
make sense. Until you're adult. Until you can climb
that mountain and know no one's really a hero. No
one. Only on television are there heroes. Until you
climb the mountain and realize. But during your teens
you're still looking. Still searching for the hero. And
drying your tears at the same time.

111

The hero.
God damn it.
The indestructible hero.

Chapter 23

I guess life had to go on. Keith and I were OK, anyway. We went out to the pictures. And then drove to a country spot in his car and got down to things a bit, sexual-wise. Well, we got into finding out what real caressing was all about. His parts and mine. Very private. Yes, but very nice. It was good. I completely fancied Keith. Much more than I'd ever fancied Ricky and that made the whole thing more meaningful and exciting. We didn't actually make love but we felt so together afterwards. I knew it was right because I felt so much at peace. All there. Completely all there. It made my worries about Tessa diminish slightly. Have some hope, I thought. Have some hope.

The next night we had a rehearsal with the band. I guess it was then that I first wondered about Keith. Well, I didn't really wonder, more worry. It wasn't until we'd practically finished the rehearsal, though, later in the evening. At first, when it was just the boys and me, without Dad, who was at the hospital, and without Mike, it was all right. We all just got into the music and this time we had the drums and everything was pretty way out again. We were recording some of the stuff to see how we sounded too. So, it was all on the move, so to speak.

When we were just about finishing, apart from a couple of numbers, Mike came in. I guess it was then that I noticed some tension from Keith. He wasn't quite so relaxed. I could notice it but I couldn't quite fathom what was wrong with him. Not until it all came out into the open. When Mike stopped us from playing and bounded up on to the stage.

'Can you make tomorrow evening downtown, kids?' he asked.

'Tomorrow?' Rod queried.

'Yeah. Special night sort of thing. OK, I've got to let you into the secret. We had to make sure you were the right band first, though.'

I looked at Keith, wondering what it was all about. He just looked stony, like I'd never seen him look before. Real cold and stony.

'The fact is,' Mike continued 'A guy from the BBC is coming down tomorrow. He wants to see the whole thing in rehearsal, band as well. I've sorted it out with your Dad, Matti.'

'What the hell do they want with us lot?' Dave said, but there was excitement in his voice.

'Well, they're doing this new series. About people who are trying to hit the big time. They want to follow us right through to the competition. Real big. We're a big group, guys. Anyway, he's going to come down and weigh us all up tomorrow night. So, can you all make it?'

There were general nods from us all. Apart from Keith who jumped off the stage and went into the kitchen.

'So, tomorrow night, then. I've got to dash. Matti's Dad will organize the transport. He's coming later. See you tomorrow then. Eight sharp.'

'Sure, Mike. See yer.'

'Wow-ee. The Beeb Beeb Ceeb.' Rod did a small dance.

'Are we on our way or are we on our way. What d'you think, Matti?'

'It's great. I'm just going to see Keith.'

I found him in the kitchen. He was making a cup of coffee.

'Keith?' I tried not to sound too excited about the news, although I really was. He didn't answer. 'What's going on?'

'Something' he sounded arsey.

'What's wrong?'

'I don't know what my old man's getting us into, that's what's wrong.'

'Well, it can only be good, surely. Whatever it is.'

'Good for who? Him?'

'Keith!'

'I'm just bloody annoyed. He's led us into it, hasn't he? I mean why would someone from the BBC come down unless he's interested in something.'

'OK, so? What's wrong with that?'

'Well, that'll be me out for a start.'

'Don't be crazy. What about the music?'

'He won't give up trying to push me into show biz. It's usually the other way round, isn't it? No, not with him.'

'You want to make it with your music, though.'

'In my own time, Matti. There is a difference.'

I sighed. I just didn't know why he was so humpy about it. Him being like that made it seem less exciting.

'Oh, Keith,' I touched his cheek with my finger.

'Sorry, but there it goes. Here's yer Dad.' I turned round and saw Dad walk across to the boys, Tracy was with him and she looked happy. I was glad about that, wasn't I? 'You are still into the band, aren't you?' I asked Keith.

'Who knows? Tomorrow's the big night. Maybe I won't even turn up.'

'You're just being ridiculous.' I was beginning to get a bit peeved with him. 'I mean, I don't see the hassle.'

'I'm just annoyed he went behind our backs, that's all.'

'Yeah, but if it was for our own good. Maybe he had to do it that way.'

He finished making the coffee and turned round to me.

'Are you only interested in making it big, Matti?'

'What d'you mean?'

'I mean turning out like your old man has. Stars in the sky and all that.'

'Well, nothing's wrong with that. We can do it together, Keith.'

'Yeah, we can do it together.' He turned away from me and walked through to the lobby. I followed him.

'I thought you wanted to make it with your music.'

'Not until I'm ready.'

'You don't then. In that case you're not bothered. Perhaps it's just a pipe dream with you. Not reality. Your Dad didn't only do this thing for you anyway. He did it for all of us involved. To me, that means something.'

'Go home, Matti. Your Daddy's waiting.'

'Why d'you say it like that?'

'Go home, OK?'

'Nothing's wrong with my Dad.'

'Well, that's a turn up for the books. Is it 'cause you got your drum kit back.'

'You pig.'

'Go home for God's sake.'

'Before what? We row?'

'I'm not theatrical like you. I don't like rows.'

'I'll see you tomorrow then, maybe. If you decide to

116

swallow your pride and turn up.' I swung away from him with that last retort and went outside, fuming slightly, to help clear the gear.

I was really in a mood on the way home. It was only our first argument, I kept trying to rationalize. It was only our first argument. What mattered? One argument. What the hell mattered?

'You're quiet,' Tracy said when we were going in. 'What's wrong?'

'I had an argument with Keith.'

'What about?'

'Oh, nothing. Forget it. He can be a pig if he wants. Why should I care? I'll do what I want. And he can do what the hell he likes.'

I didn't feel like going in the lounge with the others so went up to my pad instead. I popped into Tessa's room on the way and she was sleeping soundly so I kissed her forehead and left her. I took my make-up off, washed and changed into my shirt-type nightie. I switched my tape on and listened to 'Now there's music seven'. I thought about the man from the BBC coming down. Then I thought of Tessa. If only she was well enough to take a part in it all. She wasn't though. In the last few days her stomach had swollen badly. She almost looked pregnant. Her feet were also very puffy. She wasn't well. Not well at all. I guess I'd stopped thinking about her dying. I just tried to be with her as much as I could. I tried to be with her and talked to her. A lot about the song I was working on which was based on her life. Based on the poems she'd worked on. That really lifted her a lot. Knowing we were going to use some of her material. I joked with her that it would be in the charts as soon as a record company took it on. I was trying to make her laugh and I did so. I felt elated to see her smile

117

but in a way it was poor consolation for her illness. The nurse came once a day to give her an injection. I guess it was like I was hanging on to the fact that every day she was still snuggled up in the chair. Alive. Still alive. It was just an illness. She'll get through it. Of course she will. Christ, she's got to get through it. But then, when I watched her struggle up the small flight of stairs, I wondered. Sometimes I allowed myself to wonder. She could have slept downstairs. There was a bed down there for her and Dad would have slept down too. But she always made it upstairs. She loved her bedroom. I think she wanted to die there. That's why she struggled up there every night. I guess she wanted to die there and that thought made me cry and then I thought of my Mum dying. And me not staying with her and why I didn't. And it all got too much emotionally. So I had to try and switch myself off. Switch myself off. I thought of Keith and why he was so arsey. I hadn't seen him like that before and it worried me. It wasn't only that he had it in for his Dad, he also seemed to have it in for my Dad as well. Oh, well, what the hell's point is there in worrying. Well, work tomorrow, I couldn't wait to get through the day so the evening would come. I was excited about it. Excited. Special. Something special's going to happen. A step forward in my career perhaps. Maybe. Maybe. Something special. I could feel it everywhere.

I guess the most important thing to me then, though, was Tessa's song. Her song because it had come from her life. Tessa's song. And when I could tell her about the BBC I knew she'd be really chuffed. And that mattered a lot to me that I could make Tessa happy. It really mattered one hell of a lot.

Chapter 24

We all overslept the next morning. So, it was all one hell of a rush. Everyone dashing into the bathroom. Making breakfast and coffee. I hated being late and was in a right panic but it made it better that Tracy was with me when we got in to work and we were only just over five minutes late. I apologized to Guiseppe and said I'd have five minutes less at lunchbreak but he told me not to worry. I apologized for Tracy too because she just went to her place without saying anything. Actually, she seemed in a bit of a mood. I put it down to the hectic start to the morning, but in the afternoon I changed my mind about that.

After lunch we were all chatting and that before Guiseppe got in. Well, we were on my table anyway. I was talking to Maggie and we were joking about. Then Guiseppe came in. Now, I knew there was a girl on Tracy's table that she didn't like very much. She was often rude about her at home. I didn't really know what she was getting at because the seventeen-year-old girl called Pam, seemed all right to me.

Anyway, it was about fifteen minutes before break when suddenly all hell was let loose.

'Wanna fight, you bitch? I'll kill you.'

I turned round along with everyone else, and Tracy, who'd shouted, was on her feet and approaching Pam. On her way she swept all of Pam's work from the bench and on to the floor.

'Wanna fight? Come on then, fight. Prove yer mouth,

bitch. Prove yer mouth.' Tracy pushed the girl and then Pam was upon her and suddenly in front of all our eyes they were involved in a brawl. Clawing. Punching. Kicking each other. I guess it hadn't been going on very long before a boy called Joseph and another of the lads were on their feet and dragging the girls apart. It was really awful. They'd been like small fiery monsters. Full of venom for each other. I was just dumbstruck.

Tracy was still shouting and swearing until Guiseppe went over and shouted at her. He half pushed her towards the door and told her to come back when she could control herself. Then he took Pam to the other side of the factory.

Debbie looked at me, raising her eyebrows. I said nothing. I thought Tracy had been in a mood, but what an outburst. It must be getting to her, I thought. About Tessa. She seemed to be taking it very well. She hadn't cried in front of any of us, anyway. Perhaps that was the trouble.

'Matti.'

I looked up at Guiseppe.

'Go and see if your sister's all right, will you?'

'Yeah. OK.'

'Talk to her. Find out the trouble.'

'OK.'

I went out the swing doors and along the corridor just as the bell went for break. I went through some other doors which led outside. She was sitting on a pile of bricks, smoking a fag.

'Tracy?' I went over to her.

'Yeah. What?'

'Are you OK?'

'I'm fine. I can look after myself.'

'What the hell happened?'

'I don't have to put up with bitches like her.'

'So, what did she do?'

'You're not interested in what she did. You're not interested. Like your old man, ay. It runs in the family. Tessa's sick. Yeah, Tessa's sick, that's all I fucking hear.'

'Tracy.'

'Yeah, well, I'm sick of it. Tessa's been OK. All that crap she gives you about her step-dad isn't true. He liked her, he hated me. Everyone's always running after Tessa. It never changes, does it?'

I was completely stuck for words.

'Shocked?' Tracy's wild eyes stared up at me. 'Yeah, well, I couldn't give a shit if she does die. Another one bites the dust, ay? Another one bites the dust. Don't expect me to shed any tears. Why don't you go home and tell Daddy? You will, I know. OK, you're the lucky one. You've always had him.'

'Tracy,' I sat down next to her.

'Yeah, well, I've been the good little girl, haven't I? Nothing's affected me. You only get attention when you're dying. That's why she's dying. Because she needs all the attention. I ain't feeling that lucky.'

'Tracy, d'you want to go home? I can ring Dad. He'll talk to you.'

'Too much for you, is it? Pass the buck. You manage with Tessa all right, don't you?'

'Tessa's dying, I mean. Look, I don't know what to say. Dad's been taking notice of you. Dad's been so happy with you staying.'

'Don't you want to read any of my stuff? You pore over hers, don't you?'

It was sort of strange her talking to me like that. I had to try to fit her words together. Try to make a picture of it. Of her feelings. But, it suddenly hit me. She was right. I had been all over Tessa. I'd half ignored Tracy. She was there, she was there. Like Adrian was. But that was as far as it went. I sunk inside. It was hard. I just hadn't realized. Me? She needed me to pay her attention. Why? Me? What's so goddam special about me?

She'd stood up and was standing looking over the field. Her back to me. I felt out of my depth. Really out of my depth. I suddenly felt so responsible. As if I should do something. Say something. But no words would come. No words. Just guilt.

I jumped when I heard Natalia.

'Matti?'

I turned round and she beckoned to me. I went over to her, relieved to see her. I was just about feeling sunk.

'What's she been saying?' she asked when we were back in the corridor. I roughly told her.

'Your Dad's coming. It's OK. He'll sort her out at home.'

'She needs me. I didn't think she needed me.'

'She's putting one over on you, Matti. Emotional blackmail. She's done it to Adrian. It's all lies. About Tessa. What she said. She's just lying. Did she ask you for money?'

'No.'

'She obviously hasn't got round to that yet. Don't worry, OK?'

'She made me feel as if it was my fault.'

'Yeah, that's her tactic. We'll get to the bottom of it. Go back in and forget it. I'll see you later.'

Break was over and it was all peaceful when I went back in. I sat down and tried to concentrate on the screwing down of the valves. My mind was all over the place, though. All over the place. Everyone seemed to be blowing up on me. First Keith. And now, Tracy. Give me peace, I thought. Give me peace.

Chapter 25

I thought I would have really been looking forward to the evening. But, somehow the edge had been taken off whatever the night would bring. It was hellish. Everything seemed to be going wrong.

'You're quiet,' Ade said, as he was taking me home.

'Yeah.'

'Is it about Tracy?'

'Oh, everything.'

'She has got her problems, you know. Perhaps we've all got our problems. I don't know. Some things are pretty hard to take.'

I looked at him, wondering what he meant.

'You've got your own working out to do, right? You can't take on anyone else's problems. Not at the moment. Dad will sort it.'

'She seemed to be jealous. Of Tessa. Why the hell? How can she envy Tessa of all people.'

'Remember when you heard they were coming to live with us? You were jealous.'

'Yeah, OK.'

'Maybe it's something similar. It's going to be tough for us all, Matti. It is. Tough. Tougher. The difference is, this time we're all on the same side.'

It was almost like he was trying to tell me something. Put something on to me, which I didn't know about. That was what he seemed to be doing. Perhaps he knew what I was thinking, because when he pulled down our driveway and stopped the car, he patted my leg.

'You'll survive it, Matti. You're strong. Like Mum was. Like her mother was.'

'I'll survive what?'

'Oh, life. You know, the big old world.'

'Tonight's our big night, you know. But now it doesn't seem like it's going to be a big night at all.'

'Of course it's going to be a big night. Ride on, Matti. Ride on. Come on, let's go in.'

Dad was in the lounge. I was so pissed off I just went in and flopped down on the couch. Not even bothering to take my jacket off.

Dad didn't say anything. He was just sitting there. But he sort of looked at me. And I suddenly realized something. I guess it must have been in his look. I lurched inside as I thought of Tessa and when I spoke her name it was like a kind of squeak.

'Tessa.'

I didn't hear Dad. It was like not hearing anything. I said, 'Pardon?' He repeated what he'd said. I caught it that time. I just caught it.

'It's all right now. She's at peace. She's at peace.' Dad was crying, but it wasn't like he was crying. It was like all the emotions were pouring into me. Against me. Buffeted around.

'I'm sorry, Matti. She loved you. You gave her a lot. All anyone could.'

'I don't believe it. You're kidding. Tessa isn't dead, Dad. What kind of lie is that? Mum died, yes. Tessa doesn't die.' I tore out of the lounge and upstairs. I went into her room and she wasn't there. A bunch of flowers was lying on her bed.

'God damn it, Matti, cry. Don't hold it in.' I turned round at the sound of Adrian's voice.

'She's not dead. She's not dead.'

'She is. It's all over. Now accept it and grieve.'

'Mum's dead. Tessa's dead. Everyone's dying. I've got to get out.'

He came to me and tried to hold me but I pushed him away. Ran down the stairs and outside. Outside. And then I just ran. Across the fields. And my tears came. My tears came. I just screamed when I reached the river. I just screamed. For her. For Tessa. Whom I loved. Whom I loved. I knew it would happen, of course. I knew it would happen. It wasn't a surprise. Not to me. It wasn't a surprise. So I can cry. Because I knew. And it's easy when you know. It's so damn easy.

'Matti?'

I let Keith come to me and I didn't say anything. I let him come to me. I let him take me in his arms and I just howled like the wind against him. He held me and I cried. I knew Tessa was dead, I knew that what I'd been dreading had actually happened.

Keith kept rubbing my back and saying: 'It's all right. It's all right. I'm here.' And it was strange but I wondered for a moment who Keith was. He seemed so adult and so in control. So understanding. I wondered who he was. But then I knew. I knew and reality touched me again. Reality and grief. Shedding it. Normal. It had to be normal. Like a caterpillar shedding its skin. It had to be normal.

About an hour later we were just lying in the long grass and talking. First about Tessa. Then about us and the music. And I told him if I had to choose between life with him and life with a band I'd give up music.

'I don't want you to do that. You've got something, Matti. I want you to carry on. I love you for what you are. Not for what I might want you to be.'

'What are you, Keith?'

'I'm a policeman.'

'I understand that. I think you are really.'

'You were right. It was just like a pipe dream to me, the music. I didn't really want reality. My reality is in the police force.'

'Are you going to come out of the band?'

'I think so. Dad has already got somebody else lined up to take my place. A kid he knows.'

I smiled at him. 'Perhaps it'll all be OK then,' I said.

'How d'you feel about tonight?'

'I can't play the band tonight. I can't Keith.'

'Be strong.'

'I just can't.'

'Oh, Dad will sort something out. Maybe tomorrow. I think the guy's staying down anyway. Don't worry.'

'Keith.'

'Em?'

'I admire you because you're so strong. You know where it's at.'

'I'm not an artist, am I? Not like you.' He touched the tip of my nose with his finger. 'We'd better be getting back, ay?'

'How come you were here, anyway?'

'I came round to see your Dad to tell him about me dropping out. It had all happened. So he asked me to stay in the background for when you came home.'

'When did she die?'

'About three in the afternoon.'

'Does Tracy know?'

'Yes.'

'How did she take it?'

'So-so.'

We walked back hand in hand and in a way I felt

some kind of relief. In a way it was like not having to see Tessa ill again. Not having to see her in pain. She's with her God now, I thought. She's with her God. So, we must bear our grief, like she bore her illness. We must do that. We must do that with strength.

Chapter 26

We didn't do the music that night. Dad spoke to Mike and he arranged that we could meet the next night. I didn't feel like doing it at all. It was the last thing I wanted to think about really. It was like it had all taken a bitter twist with Tessa dying. In a strange kind of way as if I wasn't meant to play in a band after all.

The next day, though, neither Tracy nor I went to work. Since Adrian had gone to college we were at home alone with Dad and we sort of talked things out. This was going to be the night of the band. The big night which should have been yesterday. But Tessa died. And Tessa had still died. In fact it had been twenty-four hours because at three o'clock I was sitting in the lounge drinking coffee alone. Listening to 'The Sounds of Silence' by Simon and Garfunkel because it was a depressing record and that was how I was feeling at that moment. How good for someone to write depressing songs. Everyone must like them at some point or other even if they do make you cry.

Dad came down and turned the record off, though. And I felt too deflated to argue against it.

'I've had a talk to Tracy,' he said. 'She's all right.'

'I guess I'm not jealous any more,' I said. Thoughts coming out into the open, because I'd been thinking a lot over the past hours.

'Don't condemn yourself because you felt jealous of her. That was your problem. She had hers too. You helped her.'

'Why does everyone get so screwed up about life when death is just round the corner.'

'Because you can't think of life as if death's just round the corner.'

'Perhaps we should think like that, though.'

'Who's to know.'

'You should know. You were Tessa's hero.'

'I tried to make things up to her.'

'You did make it up to her. You were there at the end. That was what she wanted.'

'I wasn't there when she really needed me, though, was I?'

'Do you feel guilty?' I looked at him.

'God doesn't condemn us for our mistakes. I don't think Tessa condemned anyone either.

'She didn't, Dad. She loved you.' Because that was the truth and I felt there was no reason why he should feel guilty.

'So, another chapter ends.' And he actually smiled. Which I was glad about because he'd cried a lot last night. A lot to me. I'd hardly ever seen him cry before. And it was kind of unnerving in a way.

'Dad?'

'Em?'

'Is she happy now?'

'Yes, she's happy now.'

'I might come to church with you on Sunday. D'you mind?'

'Of course I don't. I'd love you to come.'

'Sometimes, d'you get the feeling that she's still alive? That she will suddenly come through the door.'

'Yeah, I get that feeling sometimes.'

'And then it's like suddenly realizing again she's dead. And that sort of knocks you down again.'

'It'll take time. All we can do is talk and cry. Anyway we'll have some sandwiches for tea then we'll all go out for a walk. Over to the lea. Have a good walk. It's a nice afternoon.'

'All right.'

'And I don't want to see you moping to that record again. You mustn't dwell on it. You must just let it come out naturally. Tonight we'll do the band.'

I sighed.

'Life's got to go on. Tessa wouldn't have wanted us to just give up. Don't forget her song.'

'I don't know why I loved her so much. I mean, I hardly knew her.'

'She was your kid sister, wasn't she?' He winked at me.

I nodded. Tears coming again.

'Dad.'

'What?'

'I love you. And Adrian. And Tracy.'

'I know you do. Right, you get on with the sandwiches and I'll pop down to the shops.'

'All right.'

'Make sure Tracy doesn't mope in her room for long, OK?'

'I'll go and get her.'

Dad got up and kissed me on the head before he went out.

The lea wasn't a lea really. It was like a woods and common. Hills and valleys. It covered a good bit of space and it was lovely walking there when the sun was out with a cooling breeze. Dad, me and Tracy walked along. With me and Tracy hooking on to Dad's arms. It was nice. It was really nice. In a way it was like we were there because of Tessa and it was as if Tessa was with us. Was with us. There. Walking in the sunshine along with us. And so happy. So happy because she'd finally found true peace. True peace. And in a strange kind of way I felt perhaps I could be happy too. And not mind too much about Tessa dying. I mean, I could now live my life and be at peace too. Be at peace about Tessa. It was like I didn't have to feel quilty about anything because I had loved her; although I'd felt jealous, I had loved her. Given all that was possible for me to give. And maybe God wanted her back. Maybe he did. Because she belonged to him. I could imagine that. And perhaps I could even believe in a God. Perhaps I could do that. Anyway, I'm going to church on Sunday. I'm definitely doing that. I'd made up my mind.

We walked and we talked and Dad bought us ice creams from a van there. Tracy seemed happier too and she was talking about a youth club she was going to join and a boy she fancied at work. It was all right. It was nice to be out in the open. Just us three together and, you know, it wasn't like I was jealous any more. Not of Tracy and the attention Dad gave her. Because it wasn't a threat to me, any more. Tracy was just like part of the family. My family, which I was part of too. Which I was part of.

'How's it going to go tonight then, Matti?' Dad asked when we were making our way back to the car.

I'd got into looking forward again to our big night. It made me just a bit excited sort of. Took my mind off other things.

'I'm coming to watch too,' Tracy said. 'I must see Dad sing. That's got to be something to watch.' And she laughed.

'You're going to have a laugh on me are you, miss?'

'I reckon you might be quite a good singer. That's what Keith reckons anyway. Doesn't he, Matti.'

'He is a good singer. That's where I get my talent from.'

'So, you're happy about tonight?' Dad asked me.

'Yeah. Tessa was so excited about it too. She'll be watching. She wouldn't miss that.'

'The guy taking over from Keith is pretty OK too.'

'Yeah. Keith is coming to watch.'

'When are you getting married?' Tracy asked, being cheeky.

'Piss off,' I said, then suddenly looked at Dad. Realizing what I'd said. But he didn't seem to mind.

'Naughty girl. Wash your mouth out with soap and water.'

'Tracy! Shut up.'

'Yeah, cool it babe.' Dad said, ruffling her hair.

'When are we going to pick the rest of my stuff up from the home?'

'At the weekend.'

'Right. Good. Jolly good. Can I sit in the front going home, Matti?'

'If you want. You act like a five-year-old.'

'I'm a year older than you.'

'Not quite a year.'

'Are you two going to stop quipping or am I going to have to take action?' Dad half smiled.

'The big he-man strikes again.' Tracy ran away from Dad after she said that and we both watched her dodge around the trees.

'It is all right, isn't it?' I asked Dad.

He understood. 'Yeah, it's all right. It'll take time. It's all right. Come on, lets get back.' Dad wrapped his arm round me and gave me a quick cuddle. 'It will all be

OK,' he said. 'It will all be OK. Take it from me. I should know.'

He should know.

He's my Dad after all.

Dads should know everything.

Until you climb that mountain, of course.

Until you climb that mountain.

Dads should be heroes.

That's true.

Yes.

Tessa would say so anyway. That's what Tessa would say. And I'm glad. I'm very glad.

Sad but glad.

Sad but glad.

Sad but glad.